GW01157894

Advance praise for *Monstrum*

'A magical and haunting collection of captivating stories. Lottie Mills' writing manages to tread the fine line between the grotesque and the exquisite with seemingly effortless ease. An utterly beguiling debut. I look forward to seeing what Lottie does next.'

Jan Carson, author of *Quickly, While They Still Have Horses*

'I can't remember the last time I sat down to read a book and became so captivated that I forgot everything else until I came to the end. Lottie Mills writes with great humaneness. Each story in this collection is so startling, so unique. There is a sweetness to her stories that's never sentimental. There is a sadness that's never bitter. There is anger here, too, but it's never purposeless. I was continuously amazed at how these stories ended, often with a turn toward hope. Toward human connection. Toward love. Lottie's stories reminded me of what matters.'

Claire Oshetsky, author of *Chouette*

'We were blown away by "The Changeling"; it's simply beautiful. I love the way it uses fairy mythology to tell a story about difference, disability, acceptance and coming of age.'

Katie Thistleton, BBC Radio 1 presenter and Chair of Judges for BBC Young Writers' Award 2020

'"The Changeling" challenges us to look beyond our own expectations and boundaries. Lottie's writing is a superb flight of the imagination.'

A. S. Byatt, author of *Possession*

'I was struck by the sheer verve and imagination of *Monstrum*. [These stories] allow us a glimpse into a world we may not be familiar with, and make that world live in all its pain and beauty... A book that is often beautiful, appalling and fantastical, but always utterly truthful.'

Deborah Kay Davies, author of
Reasons She Goes to the Woods

'It's wonderful to encounter the 'spirit animals' roaming through Lottie Mills' stories. There's something essential about their presence, not just to the authenticity and depth of her telling, but to the healing of our broken world. In many ways, this is shamanic work, and I'm so glad Mills is setting out early to share her miraculous vision.'

Em Strang, author of *Quinn*

'These gleefully modern fairy tales are absolutely alive with the joyful energy of difference, the prose haunting, luridly beautiful, and at times shockingly, deliciously gruesome.'

Jenn Ashworth, author of
Ghosted: A Love Story

MONSTRUM

Lottie Mills

A Oneworld Book

First published in the United Kingdom, Ireland and Australia
by Oneworld Publications, 2024

A CIP record for this title is available from the British Library

ISBN 978-0-86154-562-9
eISBN 978-0-86154-563-6

Printed and bound in Great Britain by Clays Ltd, Elcograf S.p.A

Oneworld Publications
10 Bloomsbury Street
London WC1B 3SR
England

This book is for my

family, with so much love.

I'm proud to be yours.

monstrum *n.* **1.** a divine omen, supernatural appearance, wonder, miracle, portent. **2.** an abnormal shape, unnatural growth, monster, monstrosity.

Contents

The Changeling

There were no flowers when Rowan was born.

It was nothing personal, I don't think. It wasn't a mark of hatred, or of scorn. She hadn't been in the world long enough to acquire enemies, and I had none that I was aware of.

It was fear. A deep, paralytic fear which nobody can ever quite explain. It runs rich in human blood, inherited from the Puritans, the witch-hunters, the fairy-fearing folk of years gone by. Our reaction to strange things is so ancient, so ingrained, that we barely stop to consider it anymore.

I saw it on the doctor's face as she set eyes upon my daughter for the first time. Her lips paled and twitched with a forgotten prayer; her fingers trembled as she traced the uncanny distortions of the infant's spine.

They took her blood, her saliva, they scanned her half to death. She knew the alien, paranoid grasp of gloved hands before she knew her own mother's touch, and for that I cannot forgive them. I can hardly forgive myself.

Eventually, after hours that sprawled like years, they gave her back to me.

Her eyes were what I noticed first. They were not the stagnant blue of happier children, but storm grey, with a gaze that was startlingly direct. It *accused*.

To me, the abnormality that so horrified the doctors was merely an afterthought, although even I was startled when I allowed myself to look.

The whole of my baby's upper back was completely misshapen, disfigured by two great lumps, a sort of double hunchback. The sheer mass of them had weighed upon her soft, unformed vertebrae, leaving her spine corkscrew-twisted.

They had hoped to perform an amputation of the strange shapes – they called them 'growths' – but found that they could not. Bizarrely, they were not made of the rubbery, tumorous flesh we anticipated, but a complex skeleton of sinew and bone. They were rock solid, permanent, as unapologetic for their existence as Rowan herself. I brought her home as she was.

As she grew from toddler pudge to coltish girlhood, the shapes became jutted and angular. By the time she turned eight, each one was twice the width of her slim shoulders. The bones within them seemed close to breaking through her freckled skin, which grew translucent against the strain, a stark white where it was pulled taut over joints.

It was a boy at the park who first pointed out the resemblance. Once the word was there, it was impossible to see anything else.

'You've got wings!' he cried, flapping his arms in crude imitation, and the playground fell silent as everybody cast new eyes upon my daughter.

Then, as if proffering her approval, she laughed lightly.

'Yes,' she said, as though it were obvious, as though she had always known. Perhaps she had.

Our life was an odd one, in its way. I soon forgot that other mothers did not spend time carefully cutting holes out of jumpers and school blazers, or knitting specially fitted cardigans in the winter. Other mothers did not spend their evenings guiding their children's bodies into various stretches, or painstakingly positioning the pillows for them to sleep on their front.

Other mothers were not chased by the press wherever they went.

It started gently enough – just the odd letter or email. When she was nine, a piece in the local gazette, which I cut out and pinned on our wall. 'A Real-Life Fairy', they called her, and it filled me with naïve delight. But, with a sickening inevitability, this descended into a rabid curiosity. Swarms of reporters at our door, at her school, at the park.

Rowan's reaction to all of this was unexpected – that is, she hardly reacted at all. She seemed ponderous, if anything, puzzled by the public's new obsession. She never spoke of it – not to me, not to anyone. She wasn't one for many words.

Then, on her twelfth birthday, she took a kitchen knife to her back.

She had cut deep, right through the layers of skin and muscle, and was still gnawing the metal into the bone when I found her. It shouldn't have been possible; if her choked yelps and the sick, sawing sound of the knife were any indication, she was in agony. It might have been impressive if it wasn't so horrifying.

The shape of her body had never alarmed me, but that stoic relentlessness did. It was my first glimpse of something in my daughter, something more than human. It was the start of a cold, nameless grief that seeped into my blood like anaesthetic.

In her teenage years, she developed a kind of resolve. Her body was crumbling under the weight of the wings – she could scarcely walk, and her barely healed skin bruised to the touch – but her mind remained determinedly fixed on some invisible horizon.

I caught her, sometimes, staring. Either at herself in the mirror, running tentative fingers over the shape of her wings, or out of the window, searching the sky with her mouth half open, eating the air.

Although her embraces were as vice-like as ever, her kisses as playful, her mind had flown somewhere distant, somewhere foreign to me. The thunderstorm eyes I loved so much grew heavy with an aching nostalgia, and, without her saying so, told me that she could not stay.

As the clock struck midnight on a late summer's

day – marking exactly eighteen years since the moment of her birth – Rowan disappeared. I heard her go: the gasp of shock, the tearing of skin, the rustling of covers. I ran to her bedroom, but I was too late. All she had left were traces: parallel stains of blood on her bed, scatterings of bone-white feathers and a window gaping open.

I still see her sometimes – or convince myself I do. It has been a lifetime since I raised the fairy-girl, but she is unchanged. Flying, at last, as she was always meant to. Her wings are wide and resplendent, her eyes twinkling with laughter – and she is always draped, head to toe, in flowers.

The Bear-Children

The father takes his daughter into his arms; he is clumsy and sleep-warm. Into the tiny shell of her ear, he whispers, 'Come with me, my little one.'

She follows.

Their house is by the sea, somewhere far away, and half sunk into the sand. This place is velvet; the quiet sits over everything, as thickly as cream on milk. Even the sea is gentle here – shallow for miles, kept lukewarm by the sun.

This is a safe place.

The house itself has no edges; it is all worn smooth and bleached beige by the light. There are no stairs, no second floor. It is nothing but a row of rooms, a place-to-place corridor, all melded together.

The father holds his daughter's hand as they step into the unreal half-light of dawn. They make their way across the beach, twin stumblers, tiptoed and swaying like the tide. They are in no hurry; time moves differently here.

It does not bustle along at an able-bodied gait. It does not impose its ugly symmetry upon this undulating little society.

(There are no clocks in the house, either.)

They reach the water's edge and the girl falls painlessly into the lap of the sea, her knees collapsing, her hands spasming with delight as she reaches out to chase the sand that flees with the ocean's ebb. She feels no fear; she is used to the ground playing tricks on her.

Her father smiles down at her, a lovely lopsided smile, and his eyes disappear into crinkles like the rays of dawn light. He falls forward too, greeting the ground with a splash.

He leans towards her conspiratorially.

'I want to tell you something important,' he says.

Her dark eyes are alert; he's captured her attention in a smattering of words.

'Look over there,' he says, and points back at the stretch of beach, pale as scar tissue. 'Tell me what you see.'

She looks, her mouth buckling as she turns tense with attention. When she speaks, she sounds almost reverent.

'The house, and the beach, and the woods far away,' she says; her voice, still so young, already carries the accent of spasticity.

His smile is sunlight on her skin.

'Yes!' he says. 'And what else?'

'The sand?'

'Almost,' he says. Then, trailing his finger through the air, 'Our footprints, look.'

Her eyes follow where he points; she nods in half-understanding. Gently – always so gently – he takes her hand and leads her once more out of the water.

They share the same footprints, which are not like human footprints at all. The half-touch of their feet on the ground, their tiptoed exploration of the world, has left bear-prints scraped into the sand.

'You see,' he murmurs, his voice a lullaby. 'Some people are born as bear-children. They might look ordinary enough, but really they have a wild power in them. It's said that, if they try hard enough, they can turn into bears.'

She gasps a gasp of complete belief.

'People say,' he continues, pressing through his smile, 'that you can tell a bear-child by the prints they leave behind.'

She's teeming with glee now, her muscles quaking with excitement. Unable to restrain herself, she dashes forward a span, knees knocking as she sprints, kicking up sand; she whirls in place to study the marks, and there they are, the tell-tale paw prints left so unknowingly.

'Papa, am I a bear-child?' Her eyes are so wide.

'Yes, my little one, you are.'

Then, studying his prints, frowning a little, putting the pieces together, 'Are you a bear-child too?'

'Yes,' he says, so hushed that she can hardly hear him. 'We come from a whole family of bear-children.'

He speaks so little of their family that his words feel momentous, carved into stone; she is five years old to the day, and she will never forget this moment.

'Here,' he says. In the space of a blink, he has unearthed something from the depths of his pocket. 'Happy birthday, my cub.'

It is a figurine, whittled from driftwood in his own, stumbling hands. Worn smooth, like everything here, buttery from the thousand nervous cuts, the months of fretting.

It is hardly a bear. The girl already loves it, second only to her father. She clutches it to her heart.

'Thank you,' she says. She means it.

The girl grows, as children do.

She drinks tea just like her father – milky, from a chipped tin mug. At breakfast, they have sticky-sweet porridge and rusks and tinned peaches; in the evening, fried potatoes and fresh fish, flaky enough to be cut through with a butter knife.

Nothing too sharp in her unfinessed hands, no shards to threaten her precious paws.

The days are for swimming and studying, as her father fixes the fishing nets and the roof tiles and everything else knocked askew. In the evenings, they light candles and draw curtains; then he'll sit at their rickety piano and play songs that have no names. Sometimes she names them and makes up lyrics to sing. Their music is always *rubato* – that is how they like it best. These are strange, nostalgic lullabies.

More often than not, the beloved bear is clutched in her clammy hand; she seldom lets it go, even for a second.

When the girl is eight years old, a great storm descends, and they play through the night to drown out the sound of the whole wild world hammering at the door.

'Don't be afraid, my love,' her father says. 'The sky is just singing along.'

She always remembers that. She remembers a great many things.

In the morning, the world is chlorine blue, the sea grass ripples in a new breeze, the cool sea invites her in.

Her father lets her go; this water is shallow for miles.

But the storm has changed the landscape, has churned up the once familiar seabed. Now, there are great rivulets in the sand and alien debris: angular, mechanical things altogether different from driftwood. Mementos of a different world, invading her own.

She stands, the water up to her chest. Her body is borne by the saltwater; she has nowhere to fall. She picks her way through the clutter, studying it through the rippled glass of the surface.

She does not understand the things she sees. This child knows no harshness, cannot comprehend the eternity of plastic, or the purpose of sharp metal.

Innocent hands claw at this pirates' hoard, dragging

treasures back to the beach to show her father. But he does not smile at her, does not praise her as he always does. His teeth grind shut. He goes strangely pale under the eyes.

'What's this one, Papa?'

She's holding a metal contraption, roughly the size and shape of a child's leg but twisted and thickly caked in rust. Tatters of leather hang slack from the frame, dark sinew on these strange steel bones.

'Put that down, little one.'

She does so, gingerly resting the contraption on the sand. Her father's voice is faint. She has never seen him look so haunted.

'But what is it?' she asks again.

He takes a shuddering breath, then speaks. She can hear him putting on a voice, artificially bright.

'It's a bear trap,' he says at last. 'They – bad people – try to catch bear-children and put these on their feet.'

'But why?' She has never heard anything so absurd.

He smiles a little, as though relieved by her confusion. But then his smile droops, and her heart breaks.

'To make them more like other people. Like normal people.'

His eyes are clouded with a memory, his head bowed. He looks far older than his years.

She is a clever little girl – she understands.

'Papa, did the bad people put this on *your* leg?'

His voice is so impossibly sad when he speaks again.

'Yes, my love. Yes, they did.'

He is lost in some unforgiving memory. But then a little hand passes into his vision: her tiny paw, gently covering his own. Anchoring him to a kinder present.

Her brows are knitted when he looks at her. She is small and ferocious.

'I can protect you now,' she says, and her determination is absolute.

His eyes crinkle into sunrays as he beams at her.

'I believe you,' he says. It's almost true.

But this storm has washed up more than debris, more than bear traps. As they amble, hand in wobbling hand, back to the house, he spots it – the sprawling shape against the distant rocks. It hits his chest like freezing water.

'Stay here,' he says to his daughter, pushing her aside and hurrying forward. She only half listens to him, still tentatively following along in his tracks towards the rocks, even as he moves far ahead.

He leaves a trail of wet bear-prints scraped into the sun-dry stone as he scrambles. It is the fastest he has moved in his adult life, the most hurried he has ever been in this distant Eden.

The sea is slavering around the jagged teeth of the rocks, foaming rabidly and rising at a dangerous pace. By the time he reaches his target, the water is ankle deep; he is in danger of being swept away.

He had hoped that it was a trick of the light. An empty dress, perhaps, washed up and making the shape of a person. A bad dream, nothing more.

Yet there she is, sea-foam pale with her hair plastered flat against her face, her lips blue, her chest faltering for breath. Alive, if barely. The frail fabric of her skirt swells around her knees with each surge of the tide. When her head flops, defeated, onto its side, he sees a wound, and a startling ribbon of blood trailing past her left ear.

He tears his eyes from the woman to look at the girl behind him on the beach. Wavering at the foot of the rocks, worrying her lip in her spastic mouth as she studies him. She has not seen the woman yet.

Back, then, to the barely breathing woman, and he feels a terrible surge of temptation more powerful even than the tides, an immense pressure tugging at his ribcage.

He could leave her here.

He could leave her here, this human flotsam, and allow the tide to wash away the stain on his soul. He could leave her here, and there would be no interlopers, and his universe could continue on with its perfect population of two. He could leave her here, and his daughter would be safe forever from the ceaseless rigidity of the outside world.

The twin mirrors of her eyes snap open, see him, widen even more. With a final, faltering breath, she wheezes out:

'Please.'

A great surge of grief overwhelms him, because he knows – has always known, really – what he is going to do. And what he is going to lose by doing so. He screws his eyes shut for a moment, clenches his fists, revels in the beautiful and brutal spasticity of his whole body.

And then he saves the woman, carrying her to shore in his leaden arms.

He is too good, this man. Too good for his own good.

The woman wakes to a wide-eyed child poking gently at her feet.

She doesn't mind it, not terribly. It is the least of all the pain.

Her skin is nothing but bruises; her lungs feel full of sand. When she opens her mouth, the only sound she can make is a sort of frayed shriek.

The little girl startles, then smiles. 'Papa!' she cries.

The voice sounds distant, submerged. Deliriously, she expects a flurry of bubbles to float from the girl's mouth as she speaks.

The girl staggers off in a clumsy rush and the room is quiet for a moment. She breathes in the gentle light of it, staring up at the canopy of pale stone. She charts the keen soreness of her spine as it presses back into the low, bare mattress beneath her. She can feel that she has been beaten senseless, half killed by the sea.

The little girl returns, her father trailing reluctantly from her hand. The child's grin is luminous, but the man evades her eyes, like he can barely look at her; his mouth moves wordlessly, scrambling for speech.

'Ah,' the woman croaks, with a smile. Her voice is rusty, but her social skills are as slick as ever. 'My rescuer.'

The young girl gasps, gazing up at her father with pure adoration. He just looks embarrassed, his shoulders folding in. The woman tries again.

'Thank you.' Quieter, more solemn.

His eyes dart up to hers then. They are sepia coloured.

'Well,' he says, a little gruffly. 'You're safe now.'

She can't tell if his tone is one of reassurance, or regret.

Her recovery is slow.

She can't so much as sit up in bed that first day, can't walk for even longer. Her hearing remains oddly muffled, her skin blue-bruised.

And yet she finds she doesn't mind. Not as she might have done in the unhappy before. This place does something strange to time; everything here is an evening haze, a syrupy concoction of elderflower and eggshells. She rests in her unhurried body.

She watches the girl stumble around the treeline, giggling, ducking to hide behind a trunk. Sometimes she tires, falls into a crawl, clambers along the sandy earth with her hands. Her eyes are darker than the wood. Her father, also on his knees, seizes her around the middle and hoists her into the air with a mock bear-growl.

The first time the woman steps outside, she walks straight towards them, donning a smile she hopes is inviting. The father – suddenly self-conscious – stops the game dead in its tracks, watching her. He does not smile back.

There is something particularly unreadable about his uneven scowl, the way his lip curls and his thick brows pull downward, casting his eyes in shadow. His jaw ticks, and she wonders if this signifies anger or just another quirk of physiology.

The little girl, normally so friendly, now stares with confused horror. She begins to tug urgently at her father's hand, the way children do when they need a private audience.

'Papa,' she says in an unpractised whisper that can be heard halfway across the beach. 'What's wrong with her legs?'

In an instinctive movement, the woman glances down to where her feet are anchored in the sand. She can't understand what the girl means. Her shins are rock-beaten, purple and yellow with old bruises, but the child knows that already, has never been alarmed by the sight before. Her gait is a little slow, perhaps, a little careful, but not altogether altered from how it has always been.

Baffled, she looks to her rescuer – to the girl's father – for help. His expression has changed. He seems to be repressing laughter.

Steering the child to face him, he runs comforting hands over her shoulders. His eyes, a little playful, dart up and down the woman's distant frame.

'It's alright, my love,' he says. 'It's just that she's not a bear-child, you see, not like us. That's just how they walk.'

'Oh!' says the child. Her dark eyes are wide as she

studies the woman – taking in her strange, unimaginative gait, the dull, flat-footed evenness of it. Then, all careful kindness, she pipes up, 'That's alright!' and stumbles over towards the visitor. Behind her, her father is truly laughing now, his great shoulders shuddering with it.

The child reaches the woman; she takes her hand.

'I'm Miranda,' she says.

'My name is Violet,' the woman says in return.

They shake hands.

The man is frowning again, guarded. But as he brushes past her, he speaks his name, a single syllable punctuated by a general wave at himself.

'Cal,' he says.

It's a surrender, of sorts.

One night, as they watch the child sleep, the woman becomes curious.

'Miranda's mother…' she begins, but the words falter like candlelight.

Cal looks at her. He's not so hard to read now, for all his indistinct speech and jagged movements. Time (there is nothing but time here) has been a good teacher, and she is slowly learning this new language of his body.

The look she receives now translates with surprising ease. Wryness. An almost-raised eyebrow. He glances back at the child.

'She had one,' he says, bittersweet.

'Would you like to tell me about her?'

He wheels around on one foot, leaning his back against the door frame, hands folded behind him and clutching for balance just out of sight. He regards her unapologetically. She watches his ribcage shift up and down as he takes a deep breath.

'Would you like to tell me how you ended up in that water?'

She snaps shut; he sees it happen. She closes around the memory and guards it like a pearl.

He speaks again. Not unkindly.

'We all have things we don't talk about.'

That night, he goes into the woods. He is gone for a long time.

For a time, she is happy.

For a time, she sings their songs with a sand-roughened voice she cannot truly hear; she clasps their rock-tense hands in each of her own and bares the bruises on her shins and dances in wild, unsteady circles around the bonfire. For a time, she belongs.

But she is only a visitor.

Her bruises pale, her hearing grows clearer every day. Her strides become stronger, surer, and the dark-browed child frowns at her with a renewed wariness. Flinches at her bell-clear call.

Soon, she feels a strange, saltwater itching beneath her

skin, begins to notice the growth of her hair. She craves a sharp edge, something to press herself into, something keen and real. A sudden surge of resistance inside her pushes against the viscous temporality of this place. She is wading through a dream, clawing now towards the waking world she had once so longed to escape.

Cal knows it too. He becomes guarded again, and his shoulders slump under the weight of approaching loneliness.

He fears it too, fears what might happen when she goes. Nobody who has seen this place has ever left it; nobody has carried knowledge of him, like a contagion, into the vast and unready world.

The primal thing rears up again, that same horrid urge he felt on the rocks. *Keep her here*, it hisses. *Make her stay.*

But he can never entertain such thoughts, not seriously, not for long. They break into sea foam, insubstantial against her trusting smile and pale, ravenous eyes.

(He is too good.)

And when dawn arrives, she is gone.

Out there, in the wide, unrelenting world, they bombard her with questions. Her unlikely survival, her unknown rescuer, her rehabilitation. They are hungry for it, all the hows and whens and wheres of it, all the things they could not possibly understand.

She does well in the beginning, truly she does. She is

as silent as the seabed, as stoic as the rocks which once cradled her battered body. She thinks of the man and the girl and their strange, natural home, and holds them fast inside her mind, closes the warm cavern of her mouth against the urge to speak.

But slowly, inevitably, the storm of their curiosity erodes her resolve. The great tide of their worry begins to carry her along, cold concern seeping into her bones. Secrets begin to slip through. Cal. Miranda. The woods and the sea and the house in between.

Never excessive. Never a true betrayal. But enough, nonetheless, to rouse an army of concerned citizens.

Soon enough, they descend on the bear-children.

Strange hands carry the girl away.

'You're safe now,' they keep saying in their blunt, even voices. She is horrified by their uniformity. She has never felt less safe in her life.

They push her father into a car, going somewhere else, somewhere far away. She catches just the merest glimpse of his eyes – sepia, salt-stained – before he is gone.

In her hand, she clutches a small wooden bear like a talisman.

Cal has not been in a car for years.

There's an alien nostalgia to it, to the refrigerated

quality of the air as he breathes, the surreal speed of the world outside. He frets his fingers over the fabric of the seat. His mouth spasms over wordless lullabies.

His soul has been torn in half.

He can feel it, the tether tied just under his ribcage stretching painfully, tugged further and further across the yawning miles. He keeps asking them, begging them, for his daughter, his cub, but the response is only ever an answerless hushing. His agony is too indistinct, too different from their own neat language. It is so easy for them not to understand, to dismiss each plea as just another unintelligible noise.

He presses his forehead against the window. Feels the unforgiving glass chilling his sweat-damp hair. His eyes roam the fleeting woods for a moment, indulging the flicker of hysterical hope he feels in his chest – that if he only looks carefully enough, he might see a bear-cub.

But she is not there – she is somewhere else, somewhere distant and strange.

Looking very small indeed, sat low behind a right-angled desk, bathed in stark, artificial light. Her head turns here and there, unable to resist the curiosity she feels about the straight-legged creatures bustling around her. Her fingers always, always trembling over the beloved bear – comforting him, wearing him shiny-smooth with her relentless love.

She flinches at every tick of the clock.

A woman sits before her. An official woman in a flouncy blouse, wearing a wristwatch and an uncomprehending smile. Not a bear-child, the little girl notes. An ordinary person.

'Who looks after you?' the woman asks.

That one is easy. 'My papa.' Even to say the word makes a small, unlikely smile emerge on her face.

But the woman's face crumbles into worry.

'And the things your papa can't do – the things he struggles with – who does them?'

The little girl does not understand. She frowns.

'Papa can do everything,' she says.

The woman's mouth opens, then closes. She writes something down.

'Do you… Have you ever been to school, Miranda?'

The child shakes her head.

'But your father teaches you?'

The little girl has landed, finally, upon a certainty.

'Yes,' she says, a little breathless. 'We have lots of books. And Papa knows about everything.'

The woman nods. Her face is impassive, but her lips are very tightly pressed together.

'And has he ever taken you to the hospital – to a doctor? Or brought a doctor to see you?'

The bear-child's face shadows over. This time, she is very slow to speak.

'I think… I think there was a doctor,' she says. 'Once.

But I was very little then.'

The official woman stares at her, as though expecting more words to arrive. But the girl's silence is determined – it holds a quality of finality somehow.

She resists the urge to press, to wring out more information, and the child is grateful. Instead, there is another easy, lukewarm smile.

'Now, it's quite important for us to know – has your father ever spoken to you about your condition? About… what it is that's wrong with you?'

The child does not understand. Her dark brows furrow. Her spastic mouth puckers. And when she speaks, it is with open confusion.

'Nothing is wrong with me,' she says.

Far away, her father sits on a medical table.

They break his body apart, or so it feels; he can imagine his heart suspended in formaldehyde, held up for the benefit of the theatre. The measurements of his curved spine and taut heels splayed in full brick-red lettering across some garish poster: *Roll up, roll up, and witness the Bear-Man, the latest freak of nature.*

The result of it all, the great souvenir, is a report about as thick as his thumb, his existence reduced to numbers on a block of milk-white A4.

Mostly numbers, that is – a height, a weight, an approximate age, the angles of his joints and the pace of his heartbeats. There are a few words, though. *Uncooperative* being one. And just beneath that, far more terrible:

Unable to live independently.

They shuffle the girl around for a while. Nobody knows quite what to do with her.

It's a surreal time for the little nomad, at once bleary and hyper-real, with so much change that her small body turns cold from the shock. There are creaking camp beds in spare bedrooms and pillowcases packed with generic girl-clothes. Nights spent immoveable with fear, paralysed by the dystopian orange light of streetlamps and the screaming sirens and the crunch of gravel and of other people's voices.

So many evenings spent in strangers' houses, being snapped at for her open-mouthed, table-elbowing, fork-knuckling, beautifully erratic table manners. So many instructions to her issued in a foreign language of false reasonability, so many 'boundaries'.

Soon, she grows sad and thin. She is sickening for the lack of seawater, and butter-soft fish, and thunderstorms.

They know exactly what to do with her father.

Before he can blink, he's in an airless pastel place, staring up at the woodchip wallpaper from his too-small bed. The meals here are formless things, easily cut into bricks or ladled out in haste onto garish, primary-school plastic trays. They affix a timetable to his bedroom wall, every second accounted for, a never-ending parade of 'activities'.

He can't stand the plasticky ticking of the clock and so, on his first day, he rips it from the wall and hurls it to the ground – very hard, with his best bear-snarl – and feels a great brutal surge of satisfaction watching it shatter into a thousand pieces.

The next day, he awakes to find a brand-new one ticking happily in its place.

The girl keeps sneaking out at night.

Not to run away – no such tired cliché. She doesn't dress for that, doesn't pack her few belongings, doesn't even put on shoes.

She simply stands in the shabby back garden, her neck hinged full back, her eyes swallowing the sky. The small wooden bear is clutched fiercely to her chest, against her heart. Her bare, tiptoed feet claw themselves into the icy soil.

Each morning, they find her with mud still caked under her toenails, the cold air of an approaching winter still clinging to her bones.

They ask what they ought to do, this latest set of parents, with the wandering bear-child.

The answers are cruel, barbed words like 'discipline' and 'door locks'. But they are better, thank goodness, than those words, better than every stranger whose hands this girl has fallen into so far.

So when her foster father spends an entire day clattering around in a disused back room, it isn't to create an elaborate prison. When her foster mother leads her in, it isn't towards punishment.

The room is simple. A small bed laid with fleece blankets. A frayed rainbow rug. A stack of books – creased at the spine, sun-bleached.

And all lit, overhead, by a skylight.

A glorious gap of pure freedom, directly above the head of the bed. Freshly scrubbed and streaming sunlight.

The bear-child, for the first time in a long time, smiles.

Each night, she looks up through that window, listens to the soft song of the sky. The tentative gentleness of these strangers – not such strangers anymore – seeps into her soul, and she begins to heal.

But she dreams of bears. Dancing bears, baited and chained, metal traps burrowed deep into their legs. She smells the iron of their blood and wakes with an immense urgency pressing in her chest. As though she has forgotten something. As though she has left some distant fire burning and must return…

But then there is the sky, and the humdrum noise of home, and kind foster parents boiling the kettle. And although it's not what she's searching for, not at all, it's enough to sustain her.

For a time.

The childless father is fading away.

The fight is dying out of him. He isn't even uncooperative now. He isn't much of anything.

He is a subject, a recipient, a bulk of flesh to be lifted and washed. There is no purpose now to the heft of his arms. There is nobody for him to carry. There is no use for nameless lullabies, so he allows his vocal cords to rust over with disuse.

Behind his shuttered sepia eyes, he sees one thousand little dark-haired girls with one thousand smiling sets of parents, swinging the child between them as they walk, straight-legged and strong and so very *normal*.

On the darkest night, he thinks that perhaps this is better. That perhaps – like they all say – he failed her by taking her so very far away, that he denied her a chance at humanity.

'She isn't like you,' somebody had said to him early on. 'Her impairment is less…severe. It's important that we minimise it as much as we can.'

He had hated that – 'minimise it' – but now, perhaps…

Each year that passes, he collapses in on himself a little more. Those eight-or-so years, that beautiful driftwood-time of long ago, seem more and more like a childish imagining, a fit of irresponsibility. What an experiment to impose on his child. What an awful, awful thing.

(He is too good, this man. He has always been too good.)

And when he falls ill, he is glad.

By that time, the child is not quite a child anymore – she has grown, as children do. She is lanky, all knees and ribs. She is a gum-chewing teenager.

Roaming a beach, her trousers rolled up, her feet bare, her gait gloriously wobbly still, but less, far less so, than it once was.

She picks her way around, scrabbling for shells, lodging her toes in damp sand. Her foster parents watch her.

She wheels around on one foot, kicks her way towards them, damp sand flurrying around her ankles. A memory jolts her and she stops dead—

And looks at her footprints.

She can hear his voice, rough and warm and so distinctively indistinct, can see the kindness of his eyes and his calloused finger tracing its way across the sand.

She remembers. She remembers.

But what she sees on the sand then is not right. Rather, it's half right. One foot – her left – has retained its telltale pawprint, but the other shape, the right footprint, is almost human. She has been gone too long; she has one foot in each world.

She gasps, as though hit by cold water. She takes steps – carefully tiptoed now – towards her foster parents.

'I need to find my father,' she says.

His room smells of sickness, his breath rattles.

He lies on his side, his gaze fixed on the brick-wall view from his window. With each exhalation, he sinks a little further inside himself.

'He would be absolutely fine,' says the doctor, 'if he would only *fight*.'

Cal smiles grimly.

He is fighting, he thinks. Just not in the direction they want him to.

Within a day, Miranda is armed with bundles of papers, old articles, lists of names and addresses.

It's difficult not to get absorbed in it, not to get obsessed with the half-remembered details of her childhood laid out here in black and white. Occasionally she stumbles upon things which predate even her: her father's medical records, yellow with age, dating back through his childhood; old photographs from the house; letters to her mother.

She holds them reverently, these relics, but makes a point not to look upon them directly. Places them down, so softly, off to one side. Not for her, she thinks. Not yet.

In the next room, her foster parents make calls, do battle with endless answering machines and wheedling hold music, shouting Cal's name over and over again into unbothered ears at the other end of the line. Her heart swells at it, at their ready understanding, their absolute willingness to help. She loves them for it.

Just as the dialling noises start to die out, just as the sky greys a little overhead, her eyes land upon a familiar name and, beneath that, an address. She knows – with the same utter certainty she felt when she began this search – that this is how she will find her father.

When her parents drive her there the next day, she feels an immense gravity, a memory in the making. As she stumbles towards the front door – painted sea blue – and knocks, she feels the moment being carved into her very soul.

Violet has changed since she washed up on their shores.

Her cheeks have filled out. Her hair is far less listless, and honey gold. Her skin is free from bruises and her eyes glimmer as they did only on the happiest days. They stare at her, first with instinctive politeness, then with dawning comprehension, and finally:

'Oh my god!'

Utter shock.

'Hello, Violet.'

'It is you, isn't it? Oh my god. Miranda.'

The woman clutches at the girl's skinny forearms, squeezing at the bones to assure herself of their materiality.

'It's me,' Miranda confirms. 'May I come in?'

Cal's condition continues to decline.

Good, he thinks savagely.

He lies on his back and tries very hard to stop breathing.

Miranda had half hoped for a cackling villain, some unapologetic interloper, gleeful about having brought the world down upon them. It would be easier that way to get it all straight in her head.

But this woman still remembers exactly how the girl takes her tea. She has chipped nail polish and family photos and a noisy washing machine rumbling away. When she speaks, her voice is kind.

'Your father saved my life,' she says, 'in so many ways. I owe him everything. Both of you, really.'

She smiles, a worn and warm smile. Then she seems to steel herself.

'It was a mistake to tell them about you. I see that now. I regret it very much. But you must understand, as soon as I started to tell people – about you, about your father – they were so worried, and it was so easy to think perhaps you would be better off…'

There is a silence between them for a time, but it is not a cruel one.

'It's a common mistake,' Miranda says at last.

Violet laughs a little then, because the serious, too

grown-up little girl she knew is so entirely intact before her, and she is glad of it.

'Well,' she says, 'I know better now.'

She takes the girl's hand, presses a folded paper into it. Miranda can guess, already, what will be on it – an address. Her father's address. The thought makes her heart dance in her chest.

'Thank you,' she says quietly.

When she returns to the car, her foster parents agree that they can set off first thing in the morning.

There's a storm outside, if he's not mistaken. He can almost taste the thickness of the rain on his tongue, can feel the muggy pressure in the room. Can hear the lonely song of the sky.

He is struck by a spasm of memory and flinches. He wonders if she still listens to storms as she always did, wonders if her face still looks the same, lit up by lightning.

He closes his eyes.

Miranda dreams of the bear again.

But there is no warmth to it, no hope, no life of any kind. Even the bone-deep terror of the dancing bear would be better than this.

She dreams of knee-deep snow, freezing her muscles into stiffness as she fights her way through the forest. She is following the tracks, those achingly familiar bear-prints, twins of her own; she is determined to see them through.

But when she finally reaches their end, her body turns hollow, her stomach feels packed with snow.

The bear is quite dead. His body lies stiff, his skin bone-cold even under the fur. His eyes have frozen over, as has the gentle dampness of his nose. Desperate, she scrabbles at a paw, but the soft leather pad of it is bloodless and cool, and the limb falls stiffly from her grasp. The bear's mouth is open in an empty snarl, his gums are blue. Frantic, she tangles her hands into his fur – obscenely soft, a perverse comfort even now. But lifeless, nonetheless; as dead as the rest of him.

The bear-child howls.

And awakes, still howling, the sky deep blue through the window above her. But she knows – she *knows* – that she must go, and now.

Rousing her foster parents then with a rallying cry:

'It has to be now, we have to go now!' And, met with their confusion: 'My papa needs me.'

That's enough for them. They bundle into the car and drive through the night.

Cal knows that he is dead.

He knows he is dead because Miranda is here, his daughter is *here*, and she's smiling at him with so much love and calling him 'Papa' like she always did.

And he thinks: *Perhaps this is what heaven is.*

But then, faced with his uncomprehending eyes, she begins to cry.

And he thinks: *Perhaps this is what hell is.*

'Papa,' she says again, and leans in to press a kiss to his parchment cheek. As she does so, she places something into his hands.

A wooden bear. Whittled in his own clumsy hands, worn buttery smooth by ten long years of unrelenting love.

And he thinks: *This doesn't make any sense at all. Why would she ever keep such a thing?*

As if she can hear him (perhaps she can; perhaps, in his delirium, he spoke out loud), she says:

'Of course I kept it. Always.'

He realises then, with the most ecstatic agony, that she truly is there.

The father takes his daughter into his arms. He never wants to let her go again.

She knows what needs to be done. She knows, and she sees to it with remarkable insistence, that uncanny quality of grown-upness finally coming into its own.

There is a great fuss about packing his few possessions, about bundling him into the car – still so unwell – wrapped in blankets and refusing to relinquish his grasp on the bear-child.

The journey is a difficult one, with his frailty and the rather threadbare information they have to go on. But they all make it work – the bear-children, the foster parents – and soon enough, they are in the woods again, and they can smell salt in the air.

They help Cal out of the car. He is shaking. He looks smaller now than he ever has before.

The car drives off then. They are alone.

The daughter takes her father's hand. Into the shell of his ear, she whispers:

'Come with me, Papa. We are going home.'

He follows.

The White Lion

The first time I saw Mr Ward, I wondered how I would commit him to canvas, given the chance.

He was handsome in a brutal, unappealing way. His hair was dark. His eyes were bruise coloured.

His frame in particular was striking to me: tall, all bulk, boxed incongruously into his velvet tailcoat. It would be difficult, I thought, to find the perfect pigment to mimic that shade of fabric, a blazing ringmaster crimson. None of my paints would come close.

I watched him pick his way through the crowd, dancing, strewing niceties in his wake. The showman. The lion tamer. Here, swooping to return a dropped handkerchief; there, waving a child towards the cages where the wild animals seethed.

His was a travelling fair, large and dirty: a sideshow, with a circus tacked on for decency.

It held all the usual diversions, of course: a

merry-go-round, spinning cheerily; stalls heavy and crystalline with sugared treats. But this was all a pretence, and a thin one.

All anyone really cared about, all anyone really came for, were the living exhibits.

And Mr Ward boasted a particularly fine collection. There were the animals, creatures from around the world: a python, draped on request around the patrons' shoulders; a real Indian elephant; a white lion, his familiar, a creature he had tamed so thoroughly that it often padded around his ankles like an obscene Labrador.

Then, other things. *Human* things.

I had heard only whispers of his menagerie of freaks, each more outlandish than the next. A captive mermaid, they had said. A feral child with knives for teeth.

The images had stirred something in me, a rabidness. My eyes hungered for spectacle, longed to devour it whole. I was still a child, fourteen years old. Vicious, unthinking.

I couldn't see, yet, the irony of my desires.

I had been searching for the sideshow, or trying to, but my gaze was pulled relentlessly towards that towering man in his crimson coat. He exerted an arrogant gravity all of his own. His very being demanded attention.

When his gaze landed on me, I felt it keen as touch. Without even following his eyes, I was aware of his focus moving over my body, tracing the non-existence of my hands, the place where my legs disappeared to nothing under their blankets. The ostentatious prominence of my wheeled contraption, the bath chair, absurdly heavy with its gleaming oak and dark leather upholstery.

Strangers' eyes mattered little to me – the stares and whispers had been a staple of my childhood – but his *burnt*.

The intensity of his curiosity was like nothing I'd ever known.

He approached me, smiling broadly. When he reached us, he shook Mother's hand first, before settling down before me on one knee.

'Why, hello there,' he said. His voice was carefully cheery. He looked back up to my mother, addressing her as he spoke again. 'And who might this be?'

'This is Lily,' Mother said. She was behind me, but I could hear the cloying sweetness of her smile.

'Lily.' He clucked his tongue over the word, testing it. 'What a pretty name.'

His eyes were drifting again. He lifted his hand and placed it on the chair's armrest. No doubt he hoped to appear avuncular, but the gesture felt inexplicably intimate. It was as if the chair had sprouted nerves spontaneously; I could feel his hand through the polished wood. His knuckles paled slightly where his fingers wrapped around it.

'You are quite remarkable,' he muttered, almost too quiet to hear.

He grinned, a white suddenness of teeth, and stood

back up to his full height. When he spoke again, it was in his usual, booming style.

'So, Lily, tell me – what would you most like to see? The carousel? The house of mirrors?' He leant forward conspiratorially. 'The sweet shop, hmm?'

I lifted my chin.

'The sideshow. I want to see the curiosities.'

His eyes flickered up to my mother for a split second before he gave his answer. He glowered down at me with teasing sternness, brows exaggeratedly furrowed, head cocked to the side.

'Come, now. I'm not sure that would be quite suitable. But…'

He paused, building the anticipation, dangling the unknown prospect in front of us. Ever the performer.

'I think I have something even better for you.'

He disappeared behind me, out of my sight. My mother melted away accommodatingly, and I felt his weight settle against the back of the chair in her place. I was cloaked in the thick fog of his cologne.

He started to push me, his steps maddeningly heavy and slow. The fair crawled by, all the delicious sideshow prospects sliding agonisingly out of view behind the blinkers of my canopy.

I couldn't see where my mother was. I suspected she was dithering somewhere a few feet behind – always eager to be led. All I could hear was him, breathing behind me. Humming some tune or other.

It was a long walk. He took us through the whole fair, all the way down the makeshift street of tents and stalls, until we reached a shabby row of houses – real houses, things of brick and stone.

They were unlived in, curtainless, people bustling in and out. They must have been rented out as offices for the week of the fair, the heart of the operation.

The door was too narrow for my chair. He went to try it – a rare unpractised moment – before the issue became painfully obvious. He pulled the chair back, veering me to one side of the door. I caught a glimpse of my mother then; as I had suspected, she was trailing behind us, looking fretful.

He moved to stand before me, blocking the light.

'Well, then,' he said, and lurched forward to pick me up.

It was absurdly easy for him, effortless even. At fourteen I was noticeably slight, still built like a child. And I suppose there was less of me than most people.

He slid one arm beneath my thighs, the other under my shoulders. Like a bride. I felt a foolish, futile surge of embarrassment as he paraded me through the corridors. Everyone smiled at the sight of us. How generous he was. How indulgent.

I studied the underside of his chin, the dark smear of his stubble against the white ceiling. The world jostled by. I felt us sway round corners, felt him lift my head to steer us through a door frame.

Finally, we stopped. He placed me down on a floor – bare boards, and the edge of a threadbare Moroccan rug. I pushed my weight forward, resting on the ends of my arms, crouching awkwardly to stay balanced.

My mother came in, and Mr Ward closed the door behind her.

I guessed that this room, in all its worn-out grandeur, was his office. Papers sprawled across the desk; chairs of dull, cheap leather sat clustered around an unlit fire.

I didn't even see the lion at first.

It was lying asleep in a corner, a great white bundle on the floorboards. The soft folds of its skin spread outwards, vast unwashed blankets of fur tinged dishwater grey and, in places, the delicate pink of raw meat.

There were diseased patches on its skin, sandpaper rough, where flies clung and burrowed. Its mane was encrusted with dried mud. An iron chain hung about its neck.

Ward inched forward, lips contorted into a grin. He reached out his hands right beside the creature's ear and slapped his palms together, hard.

The lion woke immediately, its legs rearing up on instinct. It stood unsteadily. It turned its head towards its master, its eyes discs of silver.

It looked impossibly tired. For a moment, I almost felt sorry for it.

And then it turned its gaze to me, and it transformed.

The lion's every muscle turned rigid. I heard the light

tap of its claws against the floorboards, iron knives emerging from the plushness of its paws as it pushed its weight forward. All its infirmities, its grubby beaten-dog look, fell away, dissolved, as insubstantial as spider webs.

Its gums peeled back, and I was confronted by the impossible solidity of its teeth.

Somewhere far away, the ringmaster was prattling on, his usual salesman's spiel.

'Meet Lusus. Beautiful, isn't he, and rare too – a true freak of nature, the white lion. Unusual even in Africa. He's a genuine hunter, this one, a killer. But I've trained him well enough...'

Nobody seemed to notice the way the lion was edging closer to me, the slow velvet swell of his shoulders as he crept – a stalking gait. The way his pale eyes were transfixed by my small, immobile frame.

He growled, a low, barely perceptible rumble that I felt in my throat.

'Oh, my goodness!' It was my mother who had spoken, an uneasy laugh in her voice.

Lusus was crouched now, right at my level and ready to pounce overhead. He breathed me in. Each tiny shuffle I made, each feeble effort at escape, he matched it, dancing, a pale shadow.

My mother laughed again. No, giggled. A dizzy, thoughtless sound.

'He likes her!'

I could see saliva congealing at the edges of the lion's

mouth. The fur there was stained dark. His eyes were enormous.

Likes, indeed.

The white lion stepped closer. His chain was now pulled taut, straining at the wall. I prayed that the plaster was strong. Everything was lost to the dampness of his breath, the hot, thick stench of blood. I was abruptly aware of the fragility of my ribcage, the softness of my eyes in their sockets.

The chain collar was buried in his neck, pushing into the keen, open flesh which had been rubbed raw in captivity. It must have been agony. Still, he fought, frantic, desperate to be just one step closer. To snap and bite and sink his teeth in.

'Looks like you've made a friend, Lily!' Ward's voice trilled out.

He, too, was all jocularity. But even as he spoke, he was crossing quietly to his desk. He perched there, still smiling, but his hand reached out behind him to grab something. It took me a moment to recognise it, this knotted leather bundle. A whip.

He knew the truth, then, of the lion's interest. In fact, I suspected he'd engineered it, a fresh torment for his beaten, half-starved creature. The agonising tease of easy prey.

The whip stayed coiled in his hand, barely visible, but that was enough for the lion. The merest glimpse of it had him seething backwards, crawling back to his corner with a low hiss, his head bowed.

I should have been relieved, and I suppose I was. But there was something hateful about the sight.

My mother was oblivious. And delighted.

'Bravo!' she cried. The room was filled with the feeble, papery clapping of her hands. 'What an extraordinary creature!'

The ringmaster took a mock bow.

'He's my pride and joy,' he said. 'The jewel in my crown. The pinnacle of my collection.'

'What do you say to Mr Ward, Lily?'

I glanced at him. There was something smug about his stance.

'Thank you.' I had to grind the words out.

He picked me up again. I felt the relentless velvet of his lapel, rubbing back and forth against my cheek. His warmth was overpowering.

He and my mother were talking, arrangements for a dinner before he left town, but to me it was only background noise. All I could hear was the low, rumbling growl of the lion.

His bone-pale eyes followed me all the way out of the room. I could still feel them on me long after the door had shut behind us.

Ward called on us the following Tuesday. He had dressed for respectability that night: a waistcoat of dark blue brocade, the gold chain of a pocket watch thrumming against his side. He was overdressed, really, for our modest townhouse – for dinner with a widow and her invalid daughter.

I wasn't at the dinner, of course. I was not to eat in company; my mother would not subject visitors to the sight of me, spoon-fed by the nursemaid, bundled under towelette rags to keep me clean.

No, when he arrived, I was in the day nursery – the door left ajar at my request, so that I could eavesdrop on the dining room, across the corridor.

Their conversation was dull for a long time. All the usual niceties, my mother's light-headed laugh.

'That's a beautiful portrait,' he said.

His voice was deep and, even here, it had that quality of projection, a showy boom. It carried.

'Lily painted it,' my mother said.

I could hear his incredulity, the upward flick of his eyebrows.

'Lily?'

'Indeed,' my mother said. 'She holds the paintbrush in her mouth, you see. She's developed a rather pretty style over the years.'

'Remarkable,' Ward said. His voice was hungry.

The conversation turned, then, to the usual trivia – art, furnishings, the difficulty of finding good wallpaper. Ward didn't push the matter, not yet. He waited. He was patient. He knew exactly when to go in for the kill.

It wasn't until dessert, until my mother was sweet and

pliant with wine, that he began to approach her seriously. This time, his voice was a low rumble. This time, I could only hear snatches of their conversation.

'And what prospects are there, really, for a girl like Lily –'

'– people who can *take care* of her, and a living –'

'No legs and no hands and yet a brilliant painter, that's something people will want to *see* –'

His voice turned commanding again, all authoritative reassurance. It would melt my mother, I knew. Any resistance she was offering would evaporate entirely.

'It will all be quite suitable, I can assure you, madam. I will *personally* ensure that your daughter is secure.'

I knew, then, what she would do.

He came to collect me just a few days later. He lifted me into the carriage himself. I did not cry. That seemed important somehow, that I not give him the satisfaction, nor make myself any more vulnerable than I already was.

The carriage's interior was upholstered in a gaudy red; I, white as a tooth, lodged in place, felt I had been fed into the mouth of one of his creatures already. That I was being eaten alive.

He hopped back out to wish my mother goodbye, his travelling coat swishing over the pavement behind him. He kissed her hand with showy chivalry, and then shook it for good measure, offering a meaningful glance. Everyone politely pretended not to see him press the envelope, packed with banknotes, into her palm.

I tried not to wonder just how much was in there, what I had been worth to her. I couldn't help thinking that the envelope looked a little slim for my liking.

We set off. Ward was opposite me, slumped lazily in his seat. He studied me through half-closed eyes.

He was tall enough that his knees brushed against my skirts where they fell over the premature ends of my legs. I could feel them jostling. He seemed to take up so very much room.

'We're off to Oxford now, and then up north,' he said. He sounded almost bored, as though the great adrenaline rush of the chase had exhausted him. 'You'll paint portraits for the customers, and others will pay to watch.'

'To watch? Why?'

He looked at me almost pityingly then. As if I was stupid. Perhaps I was.

'We'll need to have these rehemmed,' he continued, as if I hadn't spoken. He was toying with my skirts, folding them over to expose the ends of my legs. His fingertips brushed against my bare skin. Lingered there.

I could hear nothing but my own blood roaring in my ears, like so many lions.

He started on my sleeves, rolling them up past the wrist.

'These too,' he said. 'That's especially important. You're "The Handless Maiden".' He waved his hands in a half-hearted flourish, as if showing off the name for all to see. 'It's on all the posters.'

He looked back up at me then, and frowned.

'Christ, you're pale.'

He leant forward and slapped the side of my face lightly, several times, trying to raise some colour. This shocked me, but it shouldn't have. I should have learnt by then. Should have known what he was.

Then he seized the flesh of my cheek between his forefinger and thumb and pinched it, hard. It was a schoolyard gesture, but even applied casually his force was bruising. I felt his thumbnail bite a tiny pink crescent into my skin.

'We'll have to get some rouge on you,' he muttered, almost to himself. 'Can't have people thinking we're not treating you well.'

My room in Oxford was a narrow, windowless place with stone walls. It was in the basement, off what had originally been the kitchens before this house had been gutted. The distant, yeasty smell of my room led me to suspect it had once been a pantry.

The room had been furnished with something that was a bed in name only, and an oil lamp I could not light.

A man – not Ward, but one of his workers – had carried me down and, wordlessly, left me on the floor. I had wrangled my way onto the bed and lain there in the dark, undisturbed for several hours.

There was a great deal of clattering and chatter in the communal space outside, and I had to resist the urge to investigate.

I stayed still. It was perversely comforting to make myself an object, something to be carried here and there. To abdicate all responsibility. *If they need me, let them come and get me.* Pathetic, perhaps, but it was the only rebellion I had now.

I lay there until the world outside quietened down, until my muscles turned stiff with the cool air of night.

I began to notice my hunger. I hadn't eaten since leaving home that morning, and my stomach contorted now.

I made my way to the door, pushing myself on my arms. It was ajar, just slightly, so I could go through it freely and didn't have to fumble with the impossible smoothness of the doorknob.

I don't know what my plan was exactly. I had scarcely ever eaten on my own, let alone prepared my own food. But it had become abundantly clear that, for all his pretty words to my mother, Ward had no intention whatsoever of seeing to my care.

Of course, it was tempting to starve out of sheer spite. To die before I earned Ward a single penny. But I had been cursed with a stubborn survival instinct and, even then, even there, I felt I must do *something.*

I pushed my way through the door and out onto the cold stone floor of the old kitchen. The darkness was almost absolute – the only light was watered-down moonlight, from two grimy windows high in the corner.

I had not gone far, perhaps one ordinary pace from my room, when I realised that I was not alone. Something was stirring in the darkness. I could see a shifting greyness, could make out edges, angled shadows. I shuffled closer.

The lion's eyes opened. They were twin pools of nothing, stark in the darkness.

He was vast. I had not noticed it so much before, when he cowered under Ward and his whip, but here, he was a monstrous thing – teeth as long as my head, each paw spanning a flagstone.

His silence was uncanny. It rolled off him in great blank waves, smothering everything in a velvet hush, entirely at odds with his enormity, his unfathomable bulk. When he snarled, it was a silent snarl, which seemed to do nothing but draw more noise towards him so that he could swallow it.

It was painfully evident that the sight of me ignited something in Lusus, some deep-rooted hunter's instinct. Ward knew it too – that's why he had used me to bait the beast, to torment him.

But Ward was not here now to call an end to the game. I was alone with the lion.

He could kill me, this creature, without even drawing notice – quickly, before I could cry out, or luxuriously, severing my vocal cords and mangling me with lazy, ponderous, sun-warmed movements. Blithely unaware of my pain. Savouring his feast.

I forced my body to be still. I focused on keeping my breaths as shallow as possible. If he saw me move, was reminded of my hampered speed, I would be damned.

A dull clatter from the next room – boxes being toppled, and a flurry of swear words. The lion was distracted for a second, just a second, his eyes flickering away, muzzle twitching into a fresh snarl.

It was brief. But it was enough to save me.

I tumbled, let myself fall backwards into the open space of my doorway, then rolled to shove it shut with all my weight. I sat against it. Breathing. Waiting.

He did not throw himself at the door as I feared he might. But I could feel his weight, his solidity, against my own. I saw his shadow flicker in the space beneath the door. I could hear that very slight tapping, claws on stone.

I did not sleep that night. I was haunted by the ghost-white lion, by his velvet footsteps pacing for hours outside my door.

In the morning, a great flock of women descended on me, to wash and dress and peck away at me, to make me ready for the crowds.

They were Ward's creatures – like me, like all of us – but there was a kind of sweetness to them. I tried to let it wash over me, the way they would fuss over my 'lovely thick hair', would tweak my nose and call me 'gorgeous' and 'darling' and 'divine'. I tried not to notice the way their eyes skittered away from the sight of my bared limbs, the way the younger ones seemed scared to touch them, even to come close.

I had never worn clothes like these, bright satins, a corset laced tight, my hair up. At home I had still been in nursery dresses, all white frippery, my hair long and lank and adorned with a heavy bow.

They pasted make-up on my face, thick rouge, scarlet lipstick. The sort of thing I had only ever seen actresses wear.

'You've made her look like a tart.'

Ward's voice startled me. I hadn't heard him come in.

'She's supposed to be the handless *maiden*, for God's sake.'

His boots clicked on the floor as he crossed the room. He was in his costume again today, that crimson coat, the riding boots with silver buckles. Their leather was polished to a black beetle-shell shine.

I noticed the whip tucked into his belt.

Lusus was with him too, trailing behind, his snowy mane skimming the stone floor. Strange – here, as Ward's pet, he bore almost no relation to the creature who had terrorised me last night. He was made small by the stark light of day, by Ward's towering presence beside him.

Somehow, that was even worse.

I looked down at him for a moment, meeting that silver gaze. He was staring into my eyes so intently, and with such urgency, that if I had been a more sentimental sort – like my mother – I might have said he was *trying to tell me something*.

I looked back at Ward and started. He had lifted his hand to my face. For a moment, I thought he might strike me.

Instead, he pressed his thumb against my lips.

I was consumed by a violent hunger. I wanted nothing more than to bite his thumb clean off, just the force of my teeth and the pale crunch of bone.

It would be delicious. Not so much his flesh, or the overwhelming liquid surge of iron that would follow. But to overpower him, even for a second. To take something, anything, from him. And to surprise him, a delectable moment of horrified surprise. His shock would be absolute, of that I was sure.

But he swiped his hand away and my chance was gone. The lipstick left a blood-coloured smear on the pad of his thumb. He looked at it. Sneered.

'Clean her up. Quickly.'

They did.

I could not paint.

My subject – a young gentleman – waited before me, posed just so. My audience, one hundred hungry pairs of eyes, sat ravenous, ready to tear great chunks from me, ready to devour my freakishness whole.

The materials were satisfactory. I recognised them as

my things from home – paints and brushes all neatly aligned, sponges, water, the canvas placed just the right distance from my perch. Ward had spared no effort, forgotten no detail.

My jaw did not twinge or spasm; I did not bungle the paintbrush as I held it deftly between my teeth, did not send it clattering to the floor. I was tired, of course, from my nightmarish encounter with the lion, but I was not too tired to paint. I was never too tired to paint.

I just couldn't do it. I couldn't make myself begin.

The longer I stayed frozen, the angrier the audience became. After two minutes, there were grumbles. After four, people started to leave. Eight minutes, and words were flung my way. Twelve, and the words were coupled with litter.

Their fury didn't make me more inclined to perform. The opposite, in fact. I gazed at my empty canvas, enjoying the pristine ivory of its surface.

It was perhaps twenty minutes before Ward arrived. Lusus was coiled at his feet, tense, ready to spring. Perhaps he could feel his master's fury, or perhaps, as I suspected, he was simply starving.

'They say you will not paint,' Ward said.

His voice was hushed and furious. I noticed that his hand had drifted, unconsciously, to the whip at his side.

'That's right,' I said. My voice was unsteady even to my own ears. It sounded as if it were coming from somewhere far outside of myself.

'Why not?'

'I don't want to.'

I didn't know how true the words were until I spoke them. Ward was pale with rage.

'What you *want*,' he said, 'is immaterial.'

It seemed very material to me. The evidence was right in front of us, perfectly solid, irrefutably empty.

Ward's voice was hot in my ear. A few bribes, but mostly threats, astonishing in their variety. Lusus growling softly all the while.

It was a funny thing, though. Through it all, the canvas remained stubbornly blank. Ward's threats, no matter how vivid, could not conjure paint on its surface.

Even that strength of his, that unthinkable brute force, was made useless by my defiance. He could pick me up, certainly, throw me aside, hurt me in any number of ways. But he could not bring a picture into being by puppeteering my lips.

It was his final threat that made up my mind. Just a few words, hissed in the silence of the now empty hall.

'I am going to pay you a visit tonight.' His voice was low and cold. 'And tomorrow you'll find that you feel quite *differently*.'

I knew then what I would do.

He made good on his promise. In this, if nothing else, he was a man of his word.

He stumbled through the old kitchen that night, still in his costume, his ringmaster's velvet. He felt his way along to my bedroom door. Pushed it open.

But it was not me who waited for him there in the dark.

It was the lion.

I had heard the phrase, of course. *Torn to pieces*. But in that moment I gained a fresh appreciation of it, of what it really meant.

There was something shockingly literal about the stray foot on my bedcovers. Still buckled into its shining boot, the leather flecked with blood. About three feet away, on the floor, one of his kidneys lay loose and slick.

The rest of him was still half attached. His eyes were empty and Lusus licked his way through the the still-warm meat. The lion's muzzle was stained a delicate pink. He purred, a soft rumble of pure contentment.

I looked around, surveying the chaos we had created. I was no expert, but I imagined that it would be impossible to ever scrub the stain of Ward's blood from this floor. It was a deep red, but shockingly bright.

Ringmaster crimson.

It truly was a startling shade, I thought. Too good to waste.

I leant forward, teased my paintbrush off the ground with my teeth. Dipped it carefully into the mess.

And I began to paint.

The Toymaker's Daughter

Not so very long ago, and not so very far away, there lived a toymaker.

The Toymaker created perfection. Each of her inventions was a masterwork, a thing of painstaking beauty and superhuman symmetry. A selection of the most astonishing toys, the very loveliest, jostled for attention in the window of her small shop.

There were teddy bears with heavy honey-gold fur and sad amber eyes. There were painted puppets that danced effortlessly on their strings. There was a Noah's Ark, rendered in miniature, with a hundred pairs of animals in shining enamel lined up two by two.

Day after day, the Toymaker sat huddled over her next creation, eagle-eyed, nimble-fingered, with a yawning hunger in her soul to attain flawlessness. In the dusty warmth of the shop, she became a goddess; every last stitch and brushstroke felt, to her, like an act of divinity.

But she was often left frustrated, as not all her creations were so perfect. For each one that was pleasing enough to be placed in the window and displayed to the world, there were a hundred more which she shunned and kept out of sight.

Many of the flaws for which she condemned them were barely perceptible; indeed, they would not be visible to the human gaze. But to the eye of a god such as she, these foibles of creation – a paint fleck, an asymmetrical eye, an uncooperative joint – were abominations. Filled from head to toe with careless contempt, she would toss the offending object into her storeroom and close the door on it forevermore.

It was no surprise to anybody who knew her that the Toymaker's daughter was born more perfect than even her most pleasing artworks.

Her little poesy rings of golden hair were softer than the dolls' silken-thread locks, the gentle flush of her cheeks more radiant than the most delicate of pigments, and her eyes – bright blue – were clearer than any glass substitute.

Looking at the child, and filling up at once with love and awe, the Toymaker decided that she must channel this adoration into a new toy. It was to be a doll made in the image of her daughter, a testament to her beauty and her mother's love.

She spent months on the design alone, sketching image after image of her infant daughter's face, trying to capture it precisely. She spent endless days trying to match the exact shade of gold in her hair, and sleepless nights finding pigments to replicate the creaminess of her skin.

Each day, she would measure her daughter from head to toe, amending the doll for every millimetre of growth. Never – not once – did she notice the way her daughter squirmed against the restrictive touch of the measuring tape, or the yowling cries of loneliness which echoed through the shop while she was working.

A year was spent on the shaping of the body, two years on the painting of the porcelain face. The hair was the crown of all – ten thousand strands of pure gold thread, each one attached by hand. The Toymaker agonised over the placement of every individual follicle, fretting over each hair until her eyes blurred and her fingertips hardened with cramp.

By the time the doll was dressed, her joints oiled, her position posed, the Toymaker's daughter was a baby no longer. Indeed, she was nearly four years old.

Looking between her two creations, the Toymaker was struck, all at once, by a horrifying realisation.

The child was, of course, still beautiful. Growth had done nothing to dull her delicate colouring or narrow the wide wonder of her eyes. The measurements and designs had been exacting in every detail, and her body was perfectly identical to that of the doll.

And yet the two of them looked nothing alike. The child, the Toymaker was aghast to discover, was, in some fundamental way, wrong.

During these years of growing almost unnoticed, the girl had developed into something wild and strange. The squirming, yowling infant of years ago had billowed outwards into a child of most odd qualities.

The Toymaker had never heard her speak. Instead, she hummed strange lullabies, incomprehensible to her mother's ear. Unlike the placid stillness of the doll, the child writhed near constantly, her hands dancing in jerky movements like the most displeasing of the shop's painted puppets.

She looked at her daughter for several minutes, determined to absorb the bald horror of what lay before her. This child, her first and only living creation, was faulty, broken, a failure. Each twitching movement, vocal chirp, thump of a fist against the wooden shop floor, needled the Toymaker cruelly, mocking her for her oversight.

Overwhelmed, she returned her gaze to the doll. Undisturbed by any movement, the features that lent her daughter such potential were able to shine through. Her porcelain face smiled broadly; her glass eyes looked directly into her mother's.

Here, the Toymaker thought, was a creation she could love unconditionally.

For some weeks, she took great solace in the doll. For each of her daughter's cries, each treasured toy the child shattered, each smile she refused to offer, the doll was the perfect balm. Ever-smiling, ever-compliant.

There was a story unfolding in the mind's eye of the Toymaker. She envisioned finally presenting the doll to her daughter after so many years of work. Imagined that her little girl's uncooperative arms would wrap themselves softly around it, that she would, perhaps, kiss the porcelain face in grateful joy.

In the Toymaker's most elaborate fantasies, the girl even expressed her gratitude in words, offering thanks in a voice as sweet and clear as glass.

So enraptured by her imaginings was she that she did not notice her daughter's toddling movements. The girl had ventured away from her spot on the floor and into the darkened storeroom, home of the forsaken toys.

Most children would have been scared in so lonely a place, that dark forest of crooked limbs, ragdolls heaped on the floor as thick as moss. But for her it was a solace of sorts to see their sad, stitched-on smiles, to feel them brush soft against her like so many kisses.

She felt a sudden urgency to save them, to save even just one of them if she could. Her hands found a velveteen bear, slightly lopsided, his fur worn down to baldness, as if he had been loved too much.

He fitted just right in her arms.

When the Toymaker saw her daughter emerge with

the imperfect toy, she flew into a rage. She slapped it away from the little girl's clawing grasp as though it were contaminated, as though further defects could carry from fabric to skin.

Heedless of the child's cries, she gingerly offered her the doll instead. Positioning the porcelain arms for a loving embrace, she nudged her two creations gently together.

Then the Toymaker's daughter spoke for the very first time.

'No!' she cried, knocking the doll out of her mother's arms.

The Toymaker yelped as though she had been physically wounded, diving without a thought to the aid of the doll. She ran trembling hands over it, breathlessly murmuring words of reassurance into its two perfect porcelain ears.

The distressed bawling of the little girl faded into the background as the Toymaker cradled her most beloved creation.

One evening, the Toymaker was brushing the doll's silken hair. This was her habit – one hundred strokes each morning and night, that old tradition of girlhood.

But on this evening, something was different. On this evening, the hair began to fall out. Great coils of it, slaking away with each feather-light touch. Falling in a luminous splay to the shop floor.

With the frantic intensity of a worried parent, she tried, against all reason, to shove the hair back in place with fumbling hands. Then, collecting herself, she gathered the golden silk strands, and her glue, and attempted some semblance of a proper repair.

But despite her skill, her efforts were worthless. So many strands had been misplaced and so frayed was the old silk thread that even a lifetime of work could never return the doll to its previous state. It would never again be perfect.

The Toymaker wept. Hopelessly, and for hours. Then, like a miracle, something golden glimmered in the tear-misted corner of her eye.

It was with some surprise that she noticed the child asleep in a huddle on the toyshop floor, the lopsided bear in her arms. She had entirely forgotten that she was there.

And yet, even curled up on the dusty floorboards, she was something to catch the eye. Her hair, still golden, glimmered like a lighthouse beacon.

The living child's hair had grown long now, far past her jutting shoulder blades. She never allowed anyone near her to cut it. The coolness of scissors was hell to her.

The Toymaker studied the tangled mass of gold. Such a waste.

As soon as the thought had flitted into her mind, the scissors were in her hand. Looking between the doll and the child, and back to the doll once more – forlorn and balding – she felt not a moment's hesitation.

Ignoring the child's moaning and twitching, she seized her hair and cut a generous supply. Then, turning back to the doll's chair, she set to work.

In the weeks that followed, the Toymaker was more devoted than ever to her most precious creation. Having restored her hair – indeed, refined it to the exact shade of gold required – she set about supplying a better wardrobe.

She emptied out the chest of child's clothes which were kept in the back room. The girl would only grow out of them. Just another waste. With the doll, they would be safe forever from the ugly stains to which the other child was so prone.

Her every waking hour was dedicated to the doll, to the maintenance and enjoyment of its utter perfection. When the other child woke her at night with her wailing and banging and wandering around the shop, the Toymaker would soothe herself back to sleep by studying her doll. The mess and noise and imperfection faded into insignificance when she looked upon that fixed smile.

One fateful morning, the Toymaker was forced to leave her shop unattended for a moment in order to receive a delivery of small silk gowns. With the utmost care, she propped her most precious doll in the centre of the shop window, in full view of the street, where she could glance back to check on her.

As the shop door slammed shut, it woke the little girl. With an aching groan of effort, she gathered herself together from her place on the floor and stood up. Her bones jangled with the strain of it.

She had become strangely tired in recent weeks. Her stomach felt pinched, laced tight shut. Everything held a dizzy quality; her eyes slid around, unfocused. The air of the shop seemed too thin.

She found the light of the window and was drawn towards it. She crossed the shop – that careful, forward-leaning gait her mother hated so viscerally – and found herself looking up to the doll.

It was raised above her, there on the sill, framed by the light as though on a stage. She studied it for a long time.

She enjoyed the colours: the familiar golden hair, the pink silk of the gown. But there was something perturbing about its stillness. She felt it deep in her soul – nothing alive should be so still. She was unsettled by the falseness of it, by its sheer coldness beneath the painted lie of its blushed cheeks.

Why did her mother love it so? It was beautiful, even she could see that, but it had been made in her image. The colours told her as much.

After a moment's consideration, she stepped up to the window and grabbed the doll. She was seized by a sudden, overwhelming impulse to clamber inside it, to encase her own, twitching body inside the cool and unyielding porcelain. To look out of glass eyes and see her mother smiling down at her.

She did not mean to break it. She would have been justified, perhaps, in doing so, but she had never wished to. She could not hurt that which her mother loved so dearly.

The Toymaker arrived too late to stop it. The child's clumsy, insistent grasp toppled the doll out of place. It fell down, down, down, for a few sickening moments, before shattering with heart-stopping finality.

The porcelain face, so lovingly crafted, had split cleanly in two.

The Toymaker dived to her knees. Her hands scrambled, trying to make the pieces fit, but they would not, and never would. There was nothing more to be done.

She howled.

After several agonising, grief-soaked minutes, the Toymaker seized the child in a rage. Oblivious to how bony she had become, to her frantic noises of regret and apology, she hauled her into the darkened storeroom and closed the door on her.

The Toymaker's daughter was filled with a deep sorrow. For herself, of course, alone in the dark in this room of forsaken creations. But also for her mother, who sounded so very broken, on the other side of the door.

How sad, thought the Toymaker's daughter. How very sad and strange, to love a child who could never exist.

The Cuckoo

The girl wandered in at dawn, leaves rumpled in her hair, dragging her little blanket of moss behind her. She yawned and rubbed the soil sleepily from the edges of her eyes.

She looked younger than me. Three, maybe four years old. Still young enough to toddle. But I knew that, really, she was older. Really, she had been waiting out there in the woods for as long as anything had been alive.

I was on my own in the kitchen, finishing my Coco Pops. My feet still didn't touch the floor then, and I remember them bare and swinging over the tiles. The light leaking through the windows was still a sickly yellowish morning hue.

And she just tumbled in, as blithe as you like, tipping her head back to peruse our piles of dishes and our woodchip wallpaper and the clock that had been frozen, for months, at ten to three. The staticky nattering of *Countdown* in the next room.

She must have liked what she saw, because she smiled – this big, hungry smile – and set her shoulders. That was the moment she decided, I think. The moment she chose us.

She came and pulled up the chair next to me. The squawk of chair legs was loud, and I was surprised it didn't alert my parents. She shuffled herself into place, getting comfortable, and then fixed her eyes on me.

They were an astonishingly vivid shade of green, almost luminous, like leaves lit up by sunlight from behind. They really did seem to glow; and shot through with miniature bullet wounds – those pin-prick pupils of absolute black – the effect was even stranger. I had never seen eyes like that on a human being.

She fixed me with the full intensity of her gaze. Unblinking and furious. I felt a vague, consuming terror.

Then she lunged for my bowl.

I clutched at it reflexively, my fingertips plunging into the chocolatey milk as I clawed for purchase. I pulled, and she pulled; our eyes locked. But she was stronger than me. Impossibly so.

She seized control of the bowl, her mouth twitching open into a silent, victorious snarl. A little of the milk had splashed onto the table, and she launched herself towards that first, tongue out, lapping it up like an animal. Her fingers were still white around the bowl, her grip so fierce I feared she would shatter it.

Then she lifted it to her mouth, tipped her head back and drank. Great, broad mouthfuls, as though she had been starving, or dying of thirst. I could see her little throat working like mad as she gulped and gulped, her body too small, too slow, to accommodate her immense appetite.

In two seconds, it was gone, the bowl empty and gleaming. Her force had sucked out every last drop, drained it bone dry.

She looked at me again. Her cheeks were flushed, her lips newly plush with blood. I could feel a living warmth pouring off her.

She grinned. Her mouth was full of tiny, discrete teeth, glass sharp.

Then my mother came in, breezing through the open door in her dressing gown. I remember thinking, *Thank god*; remember thinking, as children often do of their mothers, *She'll put a stop to this madness.*

But, of course, she didn't.

She seemed not even to see the girl. To look at her, yes, but not to see her at all.

In her usual harried way, she dropped a kiss on the top of my head. The same as always. Then, as if on autopilot, she did the same to the girl, to the *creature* beside me. If anything seemed strange to her about the dead leaves that crinkled against her lips, the bugs that teemed and seethed inside that matted hair, she didn't show any sign of it.

The girl smiled at me smugly. Then she slid down from her seat, crawled under the table and tottered away.

I followed her. She reached the stairs and started climbing them on all fours. I stayed behind – slow, cautious.

She tramped straight into my room as if she knew it, as if it were hers. Amongst the Barbie pink, she looked even wilder, even more strange. Just this little muddy smudge, barefoot and leaving faint, dusty footprints everywhere she trod. Her fingernails were entirely black with dirt.

I smelt of plastic and talcum powder and the artificial strawberry of little-girl shampoo.

She smelt of rotting fruit, of soft, damp, dead things. I had to restrain a gag whenever she came near.

She was pawing her way around the room, running her hands over everything. I wanted to tell her to stop, but the words decayed in my throat.

She found my clothes, tearing through them, only one foot on the floor as she launched right into the wardrobe head first. She tossed things aside wildly, till the floor was a chaos of pink and purple fabric.

She found her prize eventually, stuffed in a corner and long forgotten. My old ballet tutu. She pulled it on at once, twirling in the mirror and beaming at herself. With her crust of rags and leaves, fat bugs still dropping every now and then from her hair onto the carpet, the cheery pink ruffles looked entirely absurd.

Finally, I could speak again.

'That's mine,' I said.

She stopped dead and looked at me in shock, her mouth open just slightly. Caught out. For the first time, she looked almost like a real child. Then she spoke.

That's mine, she whispered.

Her voice was stupidly small. There was something about it that made me feel nauseous, off balance – that made me cringe in embarrassment.

Then I realised that she had spoken in my voice. A perfect echo.

I said, 'Stop it.'

Stop it, she said in that borrowed voice of hers.

I, growing desperate, began to shout.

'Stop it!'

Stop it! My own voice again, hatefully frantic.

From the distant downstairs, my father called out.

'Girls! Play nicely!'

The wild girl bared her teeth at me in triumph.

In those first few days, she was very quiet. Deliberately unobtrusive, like a child after bedtime, staying stiller than still so that they don't get noticed and banished upstairs.

At mealtimes she would crawl under the table and clamber up onto the spare chair without moving it, so that it didn't make a sound. She ate only scraps at the beginning – wrenching my plate from my hands while my parents weren't looking. She would gorge herself on toast crusts and apple cores and burnt edges of potato, then lick the plate clean in a way that would have got me sent straight to the naughty step.

Still my parents seemed never to see her. Or to only half see her, to glance over at her and smile vaguely, before getting on with whatever terribly important grown-up work it was that kept them so busy.

Ours was a war of attrition. I became attuned, in those early days, to the very slightest shifts. Anything to tell me if I was winning or losing.

The first time my father laid an extra place at the table – straightening out the second set of child-sized cutlery, even as his brow furrowed in bewilderment – I knew that she had won a vital battle.

They put no food out for her – not yet – but she could play-act with the best of them, and I watched her make a great show of arranging her thieved scraps on her plate. Teasing cold sinew off a chicken bone with her knife and fork, then sipping delicately from her empty cup. Her snub nose upturned, her pinkie finger in the air. Every inch the little lady.

Looking at her, even I was forced to admit that she was becoming more present, more real. She was more defined around the edges. She seemed to have greater gravity, a more noticeable pull on the room. I was conscious of the air moving in and out of her lungs, of the table shuddering just slightly where she leant against it.

Her existence was becoming harder to deny.

About a fortnight after her arrival, we went upstairs to bed in the same way as always – me, walking hand in hand with my father, and she, just behind us, scrabbling up the steps on all fours. Panting from her open mouth, tendrils of hair dangling loose over her face.

She seemed excitable tonight, full of hidden giggles, laughing at a joke I was yet to understand.

My father opened my bedroom door. I understood.

Where my bed had once been was a brand-new bunkbed, perfectly made up. I could see my own bedding on the top bunk and on the lower bunk were new bedclothes, ones I had never seen before. Candyfloss pink.

I knew then why the impostor-child had been giggling, why she had seemed to have such a particular secretive smugness that day. Until now, she had been sleeping as a ragged bundle of bones beneath my bed. Those days were behind her now.

I thought that my father might address this momentous change, might make some reference to this seismic shift in the geography of my room, but of course he didn't. As with everything else, it all seemed to be normal to him, to skim beneath his notice.

He lifted me up to the top bunk as if things had always been this way. His hands were warm as they engulfed my ribcage. He gave me a whiskery kiss before ducking down, out of my view.

I lay flat on my back, processing my new proximity to the ceiling and trying not to hear the sound of his lips against *her* cheek.

He closed the door softly, shutting out the last of the light. We lay there in silence for a while. I wasn't usually afraid of the dark, but tonight it felt closer and more smothering than usual. Perhaps it was my new, alien position, suspended here in mid-air.

'I hate you,' I whispered into the dark. 'I hate you, I hate you, I hate you.'

The dark, of course, whispered back. It had my voice.

I hate you, I hate you, I hate you.

I would not give in quietly. I knew I had to do something about all of this – knew it as certainly as I had ever known anything.

It was a few weeks, though, before the opportunity arrived.

That summer had been a hot, drawn-out one. Even now, in September, the last residual heat still clung to the ground.

We were playing in the garden. Well, I was playing; she was…watching. Just staring up at me with those big green eyes that looked so strange here against the dead yellow grass and the pale brown sky.

I was playing with a skipping rope, and for a moment I imagined wrapping it around and around her little neck, imagined pulling it as hard as I could and squeezing the life out of her. I wondered if I would be strong enough. I wondered what my parents would say, whether they would feel the full force of this horror – or if even this would escape their notice, would have the same not-quite-real quality as a child's most vivid game of pretend.

I worried the cheap, frayed nylon back and forth in my hands for a while. She was still staring at me, and I felt, irrationally, that she could somehow see my thoughts, that she knew what I was planning.

I didn't know if I could do it.

Then I saw another solution at the edge of my vision. Across the garden, almost around the other side of the house, was our paddling pool. Sun-beaten and sagging from the heat, barely holding water, but still, it was enough. Enough for what I needed.

I crossed the garden. I still remember the way the dry grass speared my bare feet, the way the baked earth beneath it was as hard as iron.

The girl followed me, as I knew she would. I did not look back at her.

When I got to it, I stepped right in and waded across into the middle. The water was still lukewarm, even in this left-behind autumn. It was stagnant, thick with bugs and dirt. A few inches from my knee, I watched a wasp twitch and drown in a mangled, luxurious artistic-swimming display.

The girl was standing opposite me, still staring, her face a void. She was so small that the water came to the top of her thighs. Her T-shirt had ridden up a little, and I found myself staring at her navel. Like the rest of her, it was encrusted with rich, damp soil. A plant had taken root there, like the half-sprouted sycamore seeds I liked to scavenge in the park. Its white tendrils peeked out of her belly button like an umbilical cord.

I took a deep breath, and then grabbed her, knocking her down and pushing her under the shallow water. Then I held her there.

She didn't fight back, which surprised me. Her wildness, her feral hunger, had made me think that she would have the savage, unrestrained survival instinct of the most vicious animals. I had expected bruises, expected her dirty little nails, scratching at my face, clawing out my eyes.

But she just lay there, unresisting. She made her body soft under my hard grip. She didn't breathe in, of course, didn't give in so easily as that, but otherwise it almost seemed as if she was *resigned.*

She kept her eyes wide open. In all that dirty water, it must have stung, but she didn't wince, didn't even blink. Just looked at me and looked at me. It was not a particularly piercing look, not accusing or pleading or even vengeful. Just persistent.

I could see myself, a little upside-down shadow, reflected back in the glancing light of her pale iris. I watched as the shadow loomed bigger and bigger, closer and closer, its limbs stretching and melding as it reached out…

And pulled her from the water.

She gasped, a shocked little laugh of a gasp. My hands were wrapped tightly around her middle, and I could feel my fingers snug in the hollows of her ribcage. When I pulled her closer to me, I could feel the warmth of her, the shared air between us.

I wasn't sure if it was her heart or my own that thrummed, frantic, through my fingertips.

My mother rounded the corner, apparently summoned by the splashing, the general commotion.

'Be careful, girls!' she called out.

I didn't look at her, still locked in a staring contest with the little girl. She had not yet blinked, even to banish the water from her eyes. I loosened my grip but still held her in place.

Then my mother spoke again.

'Be kind to your sister,' she said to me.

This time, the girl's voice was barely a whisper, almost too quiet to hear. Less a mockery, more an involuntary reflex, a spasm of speech:

Be kind to your sister.

We existed in a sort of tentative truce after that. I still didn't speak to her, not really, but nor did we actively fight. I had lost the stomach for it.

Our parents remembered her more often at dinner, but if she was ever without food, I'd slide my half-finished plate over to her without complaint, carefully avoiding her eyes.

I got the sense that she trusted me more now. She wasn't as guarded as she had been – her stance was more open, her movements less snappish. She wasn't tame, not nearly, but she seemed far less likely to bite my hand off, or tear out my organs while I slept.

And she let me see more, too. It was a subtle change, one I didn't notice at first, but I realised that when she disappeared off to her little secret places, she allowed me to follow her more often.

I was allowed to see the soil when it was fresh, to watch her sneak out into the golden evening and turn the dirt with her hands. She showed me her trinkets, all the moulded coins and tin soldiers and animal skulls she had unearthed and hoarded. I saw her make medicines by chewing leaves into a paste and how she would rub fresh berries into her cheeks like blusher, to make herself alive. I saw the way that magpies seemed to turn tame for her, dance around her feet. I saw the way that watches stopped dead on her wrist.

All those arcane rituals of childhood, all those secret, sacred things.

I remember one evening, in the dusky mosquito time when we really ought to have been home, she bit with unrestrained force into the palm of her hand. She left twin puncture marks, two vampiric little pools of blood. A slight pinkness stained the tips of her teeth.

She held her hand out to me, totally solemn.

It took me a moment to understand what she wanted. I looked down at the fleshy pad of my own hand.

First, I tried to bite into it as she had. But it was harder than she'd made it look. I had gaps in my teeth at the time, and my jaw kept faltering at the first twinge of pain.

When I looked back up at her, her lips were hitched

into a sort of non-smile, like she was trying not to laugh. She scrabbled around her folded knees for a minute, then unearthed a sharp bit of slate and handed it to me.

That worked much better. I still remember the scratch of it, the quick flash of blazing red and frayed skin.

When it was done, I reached out to take her outstretched hand in mine. She pressed into the handshake, squeezing my fingers hard. She was freakishly strong for such a tiny thing.

I felt our wounds press together, the strange hum of mingling blood. This was something I'd heard of – read about in old books, even seen on TV – but never known of in real life. There was a weirdness to it which made me aware, on some bone-deep level, that I would never be able to tell anybody about this, never share this strange ritual with any of my school friends.

The only person who would ever understand this was the very girl whose hand I now held. My sister.

Afterwards, she seemed tired, slipping into that toddlerish sleepiness which made her look almost mortal. I put her on my back, felt her little arms cling tightly around my neck. I picked up a good strong stick and swung it in front of me like an explorer's machete, enjoying the great swish and thwack of it against the branches.

She would reach out occasionally, pluck off some leaf or other in her lazy grasp. I noticed that she always went after the ones which were still green, still held the stubborn hue of summer. After a while, I started to slow down when I spotted them, to hoist her higher so that she could reach.

I felt wild and strong, invincible against the impending gloom. I wondered if she felt this way all the time, if her power was blood-borne and now coursing through my veins.

I was still lost in the feeling when I hit the bird's nest.

It was my stick that caught it, knocking it right out of the tree with a sickening *thwack*. I didn't realise at first exactly what had happened – not until I looked down at the ruin of twigs and eggshells that lay broken at my feet.

It hit me at once, a sickening jolt to the stomach, that unmistakeable feeling of having done something utterly irrevocable. I stood there in silence, grappling with the sheer permanence of it, of this thing that could not be fixed.

My sister slid down off my back. I heard the soft thump of her weight landing, once more, on the forest floor. She slipped around me, coming to stand opposite me, the broken nest a great gulf between us.

She knelt down and I followed her. She cupped her hands, and for a surreal moment it looked like she might start to pray. She didn't, of course.

I saw that she was scooping the broken egg up into her hands. She prodded at it, teasing the tiny, half-there thing away from the broken pieces of shell. I didn't want to look at it, at the too-soft bird foetus and its little beak, smaller than a seed, obscenely sharp amidst the mess.

She stayed absolutely still. It appeared as though she was doing nothing, stunned into stillness. But I knew her by then, and so I noted the determined look in her eyes, the set of her jaw as she stared down at her hands with an ancient and unknowable intensity. A warmth was emanating from them, a surprising and welcome warmth, filling the air. Phantom sunlight beating down on my back from the darkened sky.

The egg was fusing itself back together, piece by miniscule piece, melding and hardening. As it did so, the bird was respooling, tightening back up. I had not thought the little thing could have muscles, and yet now I saw them flex and spasm as the creature folded in on itself. I could see veins thrumming beneath its translucent skin and eyelids twitching before the egg closed up.

She smiled to herself and then handed the egg over to me. It was a cuckoo's egg, mottled green, as smooth and whole as a stone. Heavier than I expected. Still warm in my hands. Alive.

We never told anybody about that, of course. How could we?

It was the first secret we had shared, this power of hers. It became our key, unlatched everything, the puzzle box of her being. She couldn't seem to stop sharing it all with me after that day. If she had been a normal child, I would have called it showing off.

It started small, as mischief always does. Lifting the dead mice from the traps at home, watching her draw their snapped spines back into place, making the tiny bones refuse and harden. Then her final touch, the strange warmth of her ever-muddied hands. Life. Setting them free with whiskers twitching.

Our mother and father would bemoan the pests, the skittering of feet which never seemed to quiet no matter what they did, and we would share a little conspiratorial smile between us.

But soon she seemed to grow bored of that. She was infinitely powerful, I knew, and she craved *more*.

So then it was hares in the field, mashed by a tractor, or badgers pilfered from the side of the road in the dead of night. It took her a long time to rearrange the organs in these cases, to puzzle together the endless mangled pieces. Sometimes she would sit there all night, figuring it out, never getting tired.

It took me a long time to learn to breathe through my mouth, to fix my eyes off to the side. To not gag at the smell or startle at the sight of her small hands slicked with glistening red.

The fox was her most audacious undertaking, her magnum opus. When we found it, still warm and bleeding, her eyes lit up and something inside me screamed *danger.*

It had been shot during a hunt, and the hunt was still going on, the woods alive with boisterous voices, overpriced boots trampling the forest floor.

I had never seen a fox up close. It was larger than I expected, uglier and wilder, all sharp features and jagged rows of teeth.

Its stillness was particularly jarring. The fox, familiar in motion, or else poised to bolt, seemed alien splayed out like this.

She sat down cross-legged and began to run her fingers through his burnt-orange fur. The occasional twitch of the wind sometimes gave an illusion of movement, but it was quite dead. A red-black bullet hole was punched through the middle of its skull.

Normally I sat beside her when she performed her strange magic, but on that day I stood back, kept my distance. I didn't want to look any closer at the fox, at the back of his head where the flesh gave way. I didn't want to look too long into my sister's eyes, afraid of that wild defiance of hers. Of whatever else I might find there.

She began her work, and I stood guard.

'There are people here,' I said, anxious, straining my ears to make sense of the far-off voices.

Her response dripped with scorn.

There are people *here.*

She spoke as though *people* were a vile thing, a repulsive taste lodged on her tongue. This was a little rich, I thought, coming from somebody who was presently wrist-deep in brain matter.

She didn't seem to feel any of my anxiety. Or maybe she did, but her ambition was so single-minded that she didn't have any sense of the danger until it was too late.

She had reassembled the fox's skull and was now lifting him carefully into her arms. He was an unwieldy creature, and she struggled. For all her strength, she was only small, and she barely had the reach to carry him.

Finally, she was cradling him, still huddled on the damp ground, and I had just begun to feel the crucial warmth when the boy stormed in.

He was an older boy, almost a teenager, with flushed cheeks and damp lips. He wore tweed and arrogance. There was a shotgun in his hand, which looked expensive, the leather still pristine and stiff.

For a second, he was startled by the sight of the tiny girl clinging to the dead fox – her hands and clothes both soaked with blood – but he steered his mouth into a sneer in record time.

He was about to speak, primed for some quip, when the fox shrieked and leapt from my sister's arms, bolting away as fast as any living thing had ever moved. Undeniably, damningly alive.

Whatever the boy had been about to say died on his lips. I watched him choking on his useless words, swallowing them down.

He tried to speak, but he had no response for what he had just seen. Nothing about this wild impossibility could be distilled into a pithy remark. The pure fear of it had stopped his tongue. Then the fear curdled into anger.

'You – you *freak,*' he spat.

Then, for good measure, he really did spit, forcefully. I watched it land, hot and horrid, on my sister's soft cheek, sliding down to her chin like an exaggerated teardrop.

He looked surprised by what he'd just done, as though some primitive instinct had seized him without his consent.

He evidently decided to lean into this newly discovered part of himself, though, because a second later he was marching towards my sister with fury in his eyes.

I don't really remember running between them, or hitting him across the face. I just remember thinking, with a brutal sort of tenderness, *She is not yours to hurt.*

Afterwards, my hand blazed. I had never hit anybody before. I didn't stay to watch his reaction. I picked up my sister and ran home as fast as I could.

I didn't try to talk to her about what had happened. I didn't know how. She seemed so profoundly shell-shocked by it. Heartbroken.

After bedtime, I climbed down the ladder and nudged my way into her bunk. I curled myself into her, feeling the strangeness of another person's cold limbs, her dirt-clogged toenails scratching against my shins. She was unyielding at first, and I almost left, worried she didn't want me there.

Then, in the smothering dark, her little hand reached out and held mine, squeezing tight. I lifted our tangled hands to my lips, kissing her warm knuckles. She smelt of earth, and sunlight, and living things.

But the next morning, I could hardly recognise her.

The place on her cheek where the boy's spit had landed had caved in, turned soft and brown like the rotted bruise of an apple. Just this big, horrid hole in her face, growing each time I looked her way.

If our parents noticed it, they didn't say anything. They didn't say much to her at all, actually, after the fox incident.

She was blurring around the edges again. Worse still – she was fading away.

Her vibrant green gaze paled and paled, until her eyes were totally colourless, winter mud. Her hair, too, had faded to the most uncertain brown, dry and brittle like dead leaves. Falling out to the touch.

Was she ever so small before? It seemed hard to believe.

Our parents were forgetting her again, but she didn't fight with the ferocity she once had, didn't even bother to scavenge for food. Her cheeks hollowed out. Her eyes lost their brilliance.

That night, when I went again to climb into her bunk, it was empty. I felt the coldness of the sheets like a gaping wound in my stomach. A great, dead absence.

I did the only thing I could, the only thing my body would allow. I ran to the back door, slipped my bare feet into the cool hollows of my welly boots, and went out to find my sister.

I tried to call for her, but my mouth found only a startling nothingness when I realised that she didn't have a name. I had never given her one.

So I just looked, scouring the forest, trying, amongst every strange, wild thing, to find the one which was mine.

The night seemed small to me in the midst of my determination, my sheer fury at this unfathomable loss. The hours rotted into nothing.

When I finally found her, it was almost dawn.

She was lying on the ground. No, she was lying *in* the ground. The earth had subsumed her; great thick tendrils of root were curling through her soft body and strangling the life out of her limbs. Strange fungi had burst through her skin and were filling the soft ridges of her ribcage and the hollows of her collarbones. Her hair was wild with leaves again. Her belly was already encased in a velvety blanket of moss.

My sister had come from the earth, and now the earth wanted her back.

I would not allow it. I reached for her, scrabbling to untangle her from the strange roots, to cut off these things that threatened to consume her from the inside out. I tore the moss from her trunk and listened closely to the non-existent beat of her heart.

I sat there, cradling her. Even as I did, I could feel her sinking back into the ground, feel the earth fighting to keep her body. I lifted her up higher, closer to me. I brushed the leaves from her hair. She felt soft and heavy, like something rotten. Like something dead.

I kept saying, 'You are *my* sister.'

Mine. Nobody else's.

I rocked her back and forth. I tried to rub life into her stone-cold limbs, like a farmer reviving a dead lamb. I took her hand in mine and kissed it, again and again.

'I love you, I love you, I love you.'

My voice took bites out of the air.

There was something odd about the texture of her hand, marring the smooth skin. Two small bumps of scar tissue, stark white. This puzzling detail nudged at the back of my mind.

Then I remembered her bleeding hand, pressed against mine. Her blood in my body.

I took my hands, still bundled up with hers, and pushed them against her chest. I burrowed my eyes shut and thought of the warmth in my sister's body. Thought of her, blazing with it, so overflowing with life that she had to find places to put it all. Eyes so green that they hurt to look at.

I thought of the sound of her heartbeat. I thought of it beating forever.

I felt the warmth in my hands, my sister's borrowed blood racing to my fingertips, boiling there. I felt my hands set her body alight from the inside. Making her warm and real once more. Bringing her back to life.

I love you, I love you, I love you.

THE PAIN

There was once a sick boy, and pain lived inside him. It seethed under his skin, looping taut around the bones like a serpentine parasite. It nestled between the hot, clammy muscles, festering beneath blankets of sinewy spasms.

As the boy grew, so too did this bodily interloper, unfurling into his spine and his shoulders and the tips of his toes.

The boy's body, though slight, was rock heavy, for the pain was a vast, consuming thing, spitting grease, lazing like a lord. The child had to carry it everywhere he went, and the creature was thankless, throwing tantrums from within, tearing up his ligaments and scraping at his nerves in a flurry of unrelenting hate.

The boy, once so gentle, grew cruel in turn. Each mark that the creature scratched into his bones, each bite it took of his flesh, allowed wicked venom to seep into his being and poison him from the inside out. The pain tore through him until his very soul was mouldering, like an autumn fruit teeming with maggots.

The boy's father, more than anyone, was horrified to see the change in him. Desperate, he pleaded with the child to share his burden. But although he heard the boy's pained yowling, and the foul curses he spat, and how he spoke of the pain-creature with the bitterness of the most hardened soldier, he could not truly understand. And the boy felt no better.

So one day, in the watery coolness of early dawn, the father bundled the boy in furs and carried him through the wilderness, until they reached the home of a powerful witch.

'Please,' the good father begged. 'Let me carry the pain instead of my son.'

And his wish was granted.

The pain crawled out from under the boy's skin, lifting from his bones and leaving him with an impossible lightness.

It ambled slowly – inevitably – towards the father. There was something primal about it, something disturbingly reasonless. More than the caustic sibilance of its hiss or the venom of its tongue, its empty eyes were a horror.

Determined, the father crouched before it. With one shaking hand, he reached out to the beast and lay soft fingers upon its scales of sinew and bone.

He screamed. It was the abrupt reaction of one who

has been burnt, but the cry contained a deeper agony by far. It was a grief-scream, a guilt-scream, rich with the full horror of awareness that this creature had held his child hostage for so long.

The father's eyes were immediately haunted, his face a hundred years old. He doubled over, hunched, crippled in that guarded way that painless deformation cannot induce. A silent tear, struck from his cheek, landed upon the beast's venomous tongue and dissolved with a hiss.

Then the pain reared forward, and swallowed him whole.

The Selkie

I remember the day he proposed to me.

It was a thick day, obnoxiously hot, each breath a mouthful of sand.

We were there at the beach with our friends, who were not our friends at all but his. They were laughing politely in a way I didn't understand.

He wore an orange T-shirt that made him look like an American tourist. His lips were slick, sun cream and sweat congealing on their bloated surface. Already, even early in the day, his nose was burnt to a shine, skin flaking loose around the edges.

And then there was the sea. Glittering beautifully like a thousand shards of glass.

As soon as I saw it, I wanted to shatter myself on it, to break into molecules and dissolve into its cool beauty. I allowed myself to imagine that for a moment, rolling the prospect deliciously on my tongue, picturing the purple concoction of my iron blood and the dark blue saltwater.

'It's not here, baby,' his voice broke in, all false sympathy.

He was rifling through the beach bag with an affected grimace, the great pantomime of the bumbling boyfriend. One of his friends rolled her eyes at me in shallow sympathy, as though we were somehow united by this failure.

I wanted to scream at him. I wanted to strip myself naked, to watch the scandalised unhinging of their jaws as I flung my clothes in his face and let the ocean swallow me, naked and whole.

I didn't do anything at all. I just looked to the sea, yearning. It was so close that flecks of cool foam were reaching up to kiss my face.

He grabbed my arm too tightly and turned me round. A very different kiss pushed its way onto my lips. His mouth felt cold and alien where it met mine, repulsively soft. I tried to shut off my nerve endings, make myself numb to the touch.

'I'm sorry,' he lied. 'I know how much you love the sea.'

That was another lie. He could not know, could never know, the depths of my love.

'You can borrow my costume!' chirped a helpful, useless voice from somewhere below.

I opened my mouth to say yes, but he shot me a warning look.

'Don't worry,' I said. 'I'll be fine.'

It took great physical effort to force the words out. My

body seemed suddenly uncooperative. My tongue was thick and slow. My ears rang so that I couldn't hear myself, and the pitch of my voice was a stab in the dark.

He began to pull me back to the picnic blanket, facing away from the water. He placed me down with a lazy shove, said, 'Get the rest of the food out, would you, baby?' and disappeared off to make the sea endure him.

None of this was done cruelly, you must understand. He had none of the sexy, swaggering malice of a TV supervillain. It had simply never occurred to him to exist any other way.

Later, when he asked me to marry him, I didn't say anything at all.

That was enough of a yes for him.

His parents gave us a house.

They were the type of family who could do that sort of thing, just give away spare houses by the handful. It was an old summer home, they said, and their smiles were conspiratorial, like this was a shared experience between us.

It wasn't. I don't really have a family anymore, and even when I did, we did not have a summer home, a winter home or any home in between.

I had heard his mother and father talking, voices hushed with false altruism. They said that it might be good for me 'to get away from it all'. That they hoped it would help me 'get better'.

I wasn't sure what, exactly, I was supposed to get better at – but their meaning was clear all the same. I had been found, in some fundamental sense, wanting.

We travelled to the house straight after the wedding. It was miles from anything, poised to flee at the end of a lonely clifftop road.

The living room was grand, all pointed plushness, with sofas which looked like they'd never been sat on, bookshelves all gathering dust. There were hundreds and hundreds of dead things on the walls – butterflies and dragonflies and beetles sprawled open-legged under panes of glass. Above the fireplace, too, a stuffed stag head with glass eyes, its mouth hoisted into an unwilling smile.

He led me into the kitchen. I felt limp and empty, my hand cool with sweat inside his. Like everywhere else, this room was dusty, underscored with notes of linoleum and mould.

'Certainly needs some work!' he said cheerily, punctuated with a hard squeeze of my fingers.

But I hardly noticed. I was already distracted. Because there, through one grimy window, was the most beautiful sight I had ever seen.

Steel grey and tumult and brine collapsing in again and again against the rocks with wild relentlessness. A violent dance, utterly stunning, utterly fearsome. For the first time in a long time, the yawning, empty hunger inside me began to abate.

'You can't swim here.' His voice was abrupt. 'It's far too rough, and so cold. It wouldn't be safe.'

I wasn't listening. All I could hear was the sea's quiet roar calling out to me across the rocks.

I swam every day – bathing in the sea, revelling in it.

When he drove off, donning a suit and a smile, down the winding cliffside road to rejoin distant civilisation, I raced to the shore. I wanted to wring out every last speck of time I could.

I had to swim naked because all my swimming costumes, all my wetsuits, had been lost in the move. I imagined them entombed in some cardboard box in a back cupboard, slowly disintegrating.

It was a sad thought. But I didn't mind my nakedness.

I loved the feel of the water, cold and close, sinking snug around me. I loved feeling the blood drain from my lips, loved watching my fingers pale and pucker, my toenails grow loose and my limbs turn blue. Each moment was a mouthful of snow, the bruising force of a waterfall on my spine.

I rolled onto my back and watched the sky turn white. A mile behind me, my dress was splayed over the jagged rocks like a corpse. I tasted salt and TV static.

Hypothermia is one hell of a drug.

If it weren't for him, I would have stayed there all day and night. If it weren't for drying my hair and painting rouge over the blue of my cheeks and swilling the taste of the sea out of my mouth with flat champagne, I would have lain there until it was too late to change my mind and let the waves rock me to sleep.

But without fail, I dragged myself to shore. Washed and dressed and made myself pretty. Cooked food I despised and ate every bite. At night, let his hands pin me, just another dead thing, against the walls.

Hated him, more and more, all the while.

Perhaps I should have stopped when I had his child inside me.

Perhaps it was – as he later said – horribly selfish to strip myself again and again, to let the sea swallow me and tumble me and drain the life from my bones.

Perhaps I really was as mad as they all said.

But I loved the ocean. I loved it with a love that was all-consuming, wild and heady, and as violent as the tides. I loved the sensation of it, the freedom of it. I was feral, with my brine-soaked hair, my missing nails, my bloodless gums and stone-chipped teeth; rabid with love, ready to scratch and claw and bite my way to freedom.

I loved it more than the thing that grew inside me.

One day, with a sickening thud of inevitability, he arrived home early to an empty house.

One day, he followed a trail of recklessly shed clothes across the rough, windblown grass of the garden, over the brutal rocks, and saw me there in the sea's embrace.

Perhaps he thought he was saving me.

Perhaps, when he waded in in his business suit, he mistook himself for some windswept regency gentleman. Perhaps, when he dragged me to shore by my hair, and then tossed me, still naked, over one shoulder, he felt every inch the romantic hero. Perhaps, even, when he threw me to our bedroom floor in a cacophony of bruises and locked the door behind him, he felt the burden of his goodness, the cruel weight of kindness towards an insane wife.

I lay there for a long time, foetal on the hardwood floor. The dampness of residual water around me grew warm, and then slowly evaporated. I felt hopelessly bereft, like a child whose most beloved toy has been snatched suddenly from their grasp. I cried like a child too – convulsively, without shame.

I shuffled, cupping my hands beneath my face. I wanted to catch my tears, every single one. I lapped them up, mouthing desperately at my palms. They were a pale imitation of the saltwater I truly loved, but they were some comfort to my gaping soul. Then I licked at the floor to capture the drops I had lost.

Hours passed. Tears weren't enough, not at all. I was in the grip of a strange and agonising withdrawal.

I rose. Banged on the door, screaming my husband's name amongst other obscenities, but he did not come. I tried the windows too, but they were sealed shut. I realised, with a sort of hysteria, that I had been buried alive here – in this hateful place of double-glazing and sensible wallpaper and upholstery in earth tones.

My hair. My hair was still damp, still carrying the water. Frantically, I stuffed a lock into my mouth, leeching at the moisture with the full force of desperation.

Then I stopped, rendered still by a moment of clarity. We had an ensuite bathroom, and I had caught a glimpse of it.

I closed the door, locked it, and then jammed it shut with towels for good measure. I ran the cold tap on full force, caring more for speed than subtlety.

I climbed inside and let the water rise, enveloping my legs and my breasts and the swollen mound of my raised stomach. Steeping myself in the freezing bathwater. I was careful to soak my hair, wetting and wringing it until all the water around me carried a hint of brine.

It wasn't enough, not nearly. It was the palest sort of imitation. But in that moment, I was intoxicated.

My body was heavy with want. I just wanted the sea, wanted it around me, carrying my weight, deadening my muscles. I wanted every cell of my body to be drenched. I wanted it more than I wanted life. I wanted it more than I wanted my child's life.

I floated in the bathtub with my eyes screwed shut and imagined I was free. But I didn't have long. I needed to act.

Without opening my eyes for a final look, I pushed myself under and opened my mouth as wide as it would go. It should have felt wrong, and yet I was euphoric. I wanted the water to touch every inch of me. Lips, mouth, throat.

I wanted it in my lungs.

A loud noise disturbed me. There he was, the hero again, clawing me away from the water's embrace.

This time, he didn't scream or grab. This time he was all sweetness, rubbing the lump of my stomach with the feeblest part of his strength.

His eyes were full of tears. Absently, I wondered if the emotion was genuine.

'Baby…'

I had never liked his eyes. They were dull, mud coloured. Even the most imaginative poet couldn't wring any vibrancy from them. Even I could not be reminded of the sea when I looked at them.

'You're not well,' he kept crooning. 'Surely you can see that you're not well?'

I couldn't see any such thing, so I stayed silent.

'Let me help you, please.' He was sobbing now. 'Will you let me help you?'

I didn't say anything at all. That was enough of a yes for him.

My son is not like his father.

He is quiet, watchful. There is something of the sea about his eyes.

I didn't love him straightaway. Not until his first bath, when his lips stilled at the blessing of the water on his forehead, when he finally, finally stopped screaming himself purple and opened his eyes as if he were seeing me for the first time.

He has never seen the sea, of course. We moved out of the old summer home before he was born. He grew up in the new house, in this awful landlocked box with people on all sides. But we talk of it often, when his father is at work. I tell him of storms and tides, of how I imagine him kicking his way through the surf and falling in, laughing madly at the roughhousing of the waves.

My husband doesn't keep such a close watch on me these days. He doesn't think he needs to. He believes he has won, believes he holds the ultimate trump card.

He hasn't realised yet that my child is not his, will never be his. Seawater runs in his veins.

He thinks that the boy is an anchor. He doesn't know, as I do, that he will be the one to finally cut me loose, set me free.

This morning, my son asked to go to the sea.

When my husband asked him what he wanted to do for his birthday tomorrow – his tenth – he grinned, all gap-toothed innocence, and replied:

'Please can we go to the beach?'

The room fell dead. There was an inaudible intake of breath. My son maintained his sunny expression, but I saw his fingers flex where he rested them on his knees beneath the table, saw him swallow, just barely.

My husband gave me a look, a warning. I am well versed in his warnings after a decade. I have become well trained.

This particular look was a warning to be silent, to not collapse in euphoria or scream or hug my boy. To not even think. I didn't move an inch.

But, to my eternal surprise, my husband broke the silence with a smile.

'The beach it is!' he said, ruffling the boy's hair, every inch the indulgent patriarch. 'We'll go first thing tomorrow morning.'

My son looked me in the eye, solemn, and gave a barely perceptible nod. I have never loved him more than I did at that moment. I didn't know I was capable of loving any human thing so much.

My husband breezed towards the front door for work, puffed up with pride. As he left, he spoke to me; or rather, he spoke at me, as is his custom.

'Get the beach things ready,' he said indifferently. 'They're in the airing cupboard.'

I did as I was told, only after I had vacuumed the floors and cleaned the kitchen and planned dinner. Only then did I make my way to the cupboard, as directed, and unearth the beach bag from so long ago.

It was dusty, of course. We have had no need of swimming things till now. I didn't even know we still had them.

There isn't even a bathtub in this house.

The truth unfurled slowly, like a memory. I rifled through the stale contents of the bag, pushing past the out-of-date sun cream, the hated orange T-shirt, long-forgotten books with sand still encrusted between their pages.

And there – just there, beneath my hand – was the truth, rendered in soft neoprene. A swimsuit, my swimsuit. Packed and unused. For the first time in years, I felt the beginnings of rage, real rage, rising in me with the discovery of this very old lie.

It was an innocuous thing, to be sure. But a reminder, material proof, of his crimes, everything he had stolen from me – or tried to.

Tonight, for the first time in a long time, I will go to sleep with a smile on my face.

Tomorrow, I will sit side by side with my son on the beach. I will tangle my fingers with his on the hot summer sand and whisper to him that, somehow, we will find each other again. I will kiss him goodbye.

Tomorrow, I will slip out of view, lost in the holiday crowds, and collapse at last into the sea's cold embrace. Tomorrow, I will swim far away.

Tomorrow, I will not be returning.

The Mirror

The girl makes her way towards the villa. She carries two large paper bags packed with groceries, and a bouquet of sunflowers still green in the middle.

It's a hot day – the spongy, oppressive sort of heat that packs your lungs and smothers thought altogether – and yet she seems impervious to it, looking for all the world as though she is greatly enjoying the spearing rays of sun, the overwhelming perfume of dust rising from this little road. And although the bags are heavy and unwieldy in her arms, she does not appear to struggle in the slightest. She's deceptively strong, this girl.

The villa rises before her as a great block of shade. It's eggshell coloured, with a terracotta roof, and covered all over in vines and tiny, spidery paint cracks. It's taller by far than any building nearby, and the overall effect of it might be intimidating to some other visitor – but not to this girl. This girl is not the sort to be intimidated. She bounces lightly up the stone steps to the doorway and puts down one of the bags, carefully, as though easing a child off her hip to the floor.

The door knocker is a coiled, tangled snake, rendered in dull bronze. Her fingertips dance over it for a second before she knocks.

With a soft cry of hinges, the door swings open of its own accord, and she steps immediately into the cool, shadowed mouth of that strange place.

They keep it very dark inside. Though her eyes are sharp, it takes them a good while to adjust. There's something mausoleum-like about the shuttered windows, the bare stone walls, the way the marble floors seem to leach all the heat from the air. The slapping of her plimsolls echoes, stupidly loud, as she makes her way down the corridor.

The kitchen is a little lighter, though, and pleasantly spacious, and an ease settles upon her as she gets to work. Filling a large tin jug with lukewarm water for the sunflowers, placing them in the middle of the dark oak dining table. Then unpacking the food: thick milk in a glass bottle; hard cheese; dark, richly seeded bread; cured meats; a huge jar of olives, cool and heavy in her hands. Fresh fruits she'd picked out from the market – pomegranates, grapes, apricots – sweet even to look at, even to smell on her skin. She stocks the larder carefully, neatly; there is a strange satisfaction to the perfect stacking of bags of rice, flour, bottles of rich gold oil.

When she is done, she throws away the bags, along with the cut stems from the flowers, and wipes down the counters a little, although this is not expected of her. As always, there is a parchment envelope left on a side table, fat with neatly folded notes, somehow always more than she expects. They pay her generously for the supplies, and the same twice over for her time.

Nestled beside the notes is a slip of parchment covered in black, spidery handwriting: a list of supplies for next week. No other instructions, no greeting of any sort, all suitably enigmatic. The girl catches herself wondering if this is her employer's handwriting or that of some other intermediary. How much secrecy, she thinks, hangs between them, like a many-layered veil?

Nevertheless, she pockets the envelope and surveys the kitchen from the doorway. Apart from the bright yellow smudge of the sunflowers, she has left almost no mark – you would not be able to tell that anyone had been here. She gets the impression that this is exactly her employer's design, that this is how she's *supposed* to behave.

She makes her way back down the corridor, opens the front door and is swallowed whole by the blazing, burning light. By now, it is the hottest part of the afternoon. She sets her shoulders and begins the long walk home, back into the world of the living.

As she walks away, she looks back – the oldest of all sins – to the villa. She sees, or thinks she sees, a twitching, the briefest flicker of a figure in the dark eye of an upstairs window. But just as quickly, it is gone. Perhaps it was only a shadow.

The next Saturday, she steps into the kitchen to find that there is someone already there. A woman with her back turned, facing the sink. It is an astonishing sight in so silent a place. The subtle rise and fall of the woman's shoulders as she breathes is jarring, at odds with the cool solidity of the villa's air, the general deadness of the surroundings.

Nevertheless, the girl steps a little further into the room, determined to remain undaunted.

'Hello,' she says.

In the faltering second before the woman turns around, the girl wonders if she is about to meet her employer. If she is about to see the face that, down in the village, has become a superstition of its own; if she alone will learn at once the full and dreadful truth, be assaulted by scales and snakes and unspeakable deformity.

A question bubbles hysterically into her mind, half serious: *Am I about to be turned to stone?*

But when the woman faces her, she finds herself at once relieved and disappointed, for this is not the monster of local legend.

For one thing, she's too old – at least middle-aged, her dark hair shot through with grey. The true lady of the house, she knows, is a young woman not much older than herself.

She is dressed simply in dark grey silk, her hair in a sensible bun. There are kind crinkles around her eyes and there is the slightest smile on her lips, at once pleasant and cryptic. She is making tea, feeling her way along the kitchen counter, guiding her hands carefully to the kettle.

Of course, the girl thinks. *Of course she would be blind.*

'You must be Maia,' the woman says, smiling that unknowable smile. Her voice is rich and deep; the room rumbles with it. It's not a local voice, Maia notices, but foreign, lightly accented. English, maybe.

'I am.'

The woman steps forward, offering her hand.

'I am Mrs Shepherd. I am the housekeeper here, and lady's maid to your employer.'

The language of it all is decadently old-fashioned, so alien to the village girl who wanders barefoot in the grocer's and takes the early-morning bus to college three days a week.

They shake hands.

'My lady wished to thank you for the sunflowers,' Mrs Shepherd says. 'She enjoyed them very much.'

'Oh,' Maia says. Then that generational reflex, 'No problem.'

A nervous quiet falls over the kitchen. When the housekeeper finally speaks again, her voice is slightly too high, almost strangled.

'Why did you do it?'

'I'm sorry?'

'The – the flowers,' the housekeeper falters. 'They were not on the list. They were not…budgeted for. Nobody asked you to buy them.'

'No.'

'So why did you?'

Maia thinks she can hear some sort of desperation in Mrs Shepherd's voice; she is fairly certain that she isn't imagining it.

'I thought it would be…nice,' she finishes weakly.

A scoff of incredulity.

'Nice?'

'I thought she might – I don't know – like them. That they might make her happy.'

Mrs Shepherd turns away, so that Maia cannot see her face, and her shoulders are set into hard lines as she speaks again.

'You would show such consideration to a monster?'

'Well,' the girl says, and smiles. 'Monsters are people too.'

She brings a gift every week after that. Some sort of defiant, bloody-minded kindness has possessed her, and she will not be deterred from her new mission. So she begins her assault of rose-scented soaps and great, smooth blocks of milk chocolate; of glossy travel magazines and orange-tinted bottles of sticky-sweet kumquat liqueur. Tokens as tiny as bullets.

Whenever she sees Mrs Shepherd – which is more and more often as the weeks go on – the housekeeper holds that same expression of guarded incomprehension, a wounded-animal suspicion that breaks Maia's heart a little.

One day, the housekeeper asks:

'What do you know, exactly, about the family? About my lady's…condition?'

Oh, Maia thinks, *oh, the poor woman. She thinks that I don't know. That I must not understand the full extent of it.* So she smiles, a little slyly perhaps, and says:

'My grandfather was a professor of classics, mythology. He was fascinated by the stories surrounding this family, to the extent that he left his university, his city, and moved to the village to continue his research into them.'

The housekeeper stares dumbly. Maia continues.

'He was regarded as a little eccentric, as you can imagine. But I loved him. I spent every single summer here when I was growing up. And after my parents died, I moved in full time.

'I have lived in the shadow of this house for more than ten years now. I have been schooled here. I have befriended the village children. I have read every book in my grandfather's library and studied every artefact in his collection and dined with him every single night. I have served drinks at the taverna and have listened to all the local chatter. There is no story I have not heard.'

'And you're not frightened?'

'No!' says Maia. A quick gasp of a response, almost a laugh. Then again, more solemnly, 'No'.

The housekeeper swallows hard and shuffles in place. When she finally gathers herself and begins to speak, the words rush and stumble from her lips.

'My lady would like to meet you. Not – not this afternoon. But perhaps next week? She gets lonely out here. I can only provide so much company.' Here, she chuckles self-deprecatingly.

Then she seems to cringe in on herself.

'I should say, of course, that you don't have to. You don't have to do anything you don't want to. That's – that's very important to her. You can keep coming here, just as you have been. Your job is safe. This isn't – that is, it's not *expected* of you.'

'I want to,' Maia says before the air has even stilled.

The words arrive so quickly that they seem to be a reflex, bypassing thought entirely. They land heavily in the room with an air of inevitability, even predestination. Maia has the oddest sensation of déjà vu, as though this conversation has always been happening, since the moment she was born, as though her acquiescence was written into her very body and has been waiting, all this time, just behind her lips.

'Yes. I want to meet her.'

When she arrives the following week, she sees Mrs

Shepherd's pale form hovering at the ground-floor window. When she reaches the door, the housekeeper opens it before she can knock. *She must have been listening for my footsteps*, Maia thinks.

'You're here,' Mrs Shepherd says unnecessarily. She sounds breathless.

Maia furrows her brows in a display of innocent confusion which is only slightly put on.

'Of course,' she says. They stand there a moment, lodged on the doorstep, neither of them daring to move, before Maia says, 'May I come in, then?'

Mrs Shepherd shuffles aside and Maia steps through into the cool, church-like air of the hall. As always, she is carrying supplies, although just a single bag today. The housekeeper takes it without asking and rushes through to the kitchen, already unpacking by the time Maia gets there.

'I'll sort these,' she says. 'You just…head straight through.'

She waves her arm vaguely towards the corner of the kitchen. The attempt at casualness looks ill-fitting on so precise a woman.

Maia crosses the room with a confidence she doesn't entirely feel. *Walk like you know where you're going*, her grandfather had once told her, *and don't give anyone a chance to question you.*

So she marches directly towards the shadowy opening of the door she has never seen unlocked, and, if she falters, it is for so brief a moment that even Mrs Shepherd's sharp ears do not notice it.

And then she is in the darkness.

The corridor is hung with great heavy tapestries, so that it feels enclosed and airless in a way the other rooms don't.

Maia's fingers brush the rich fabrics. She feels exactly like she did as a child on a school trip to the museum, sneaking a curious hand under the barrier to run her fingers along some sarcophagus or unthinkably ancient contortion of marble. Scolded fiercely for her crime. Committing it again the second the teacher's back was turned.

The tapestries here have the same sensation to them, that odd hum of ancientness. Heavy with the ghost hands of a thousand ancestors, no part of them left untouched.

The corridor opens into a small bedchamber. An obscure room, crowded with mahogany furniture packed in at odd angles. It is all corners, all hiding places.

The only light in the room is trickling through a screen, a dense sort of wooden grille – like the wall of a confessional, but less penetrable. The gaps of light between its chainmail chinks have a hazy quality, and, coming closer, Maia can see that there are layers of gauzy fabric pinned to the far side of the screen. Even the slightest glimpse is an impossibility.

A chair has been put out for her, facing the screen at a conversational angle. She eases herself into it, and the protesting creak is deafening.

Everything is intensified here. Maia is hyper-aware of her dress nudging against her skin, the little hairs sweat-damp and sticking to the back of her neck.

And, of course, the steady rhythm from the other side of the screen. A sound which takes her a moment to recognise. Breathing. If she sits very still and focuses, she can feel it through the screen, soft on her face.

There is a monster in this house, and her breath is warm.

It has been a long time indeed since she last attended confession – not since she was a child, before her parents died – and yet, in her memory, it never seemed as holy as *this*: this moment of anticipation between them. The silence is as heavy as the Earth. Maia is struck, again, by an all-consuming awareness that this is where she has always been heading, that no matter which choices she made, they would always have led her here, to this chair, not three feet away from the monster of legend.

And then, the monster speaks.

'Hello,' she says. 'You must be Maia.'

Her voice is higher than Maia's and painfully young. It's well spoken in a way that sounds almost rehearsed. The accent is hard to place, because it is entirely its own. The signature dialect of a nation of one.

'Hello,' Maia replies.

All at once, she's forgotten every conversation she's ever had. She feels a sudden, stupid instinct to return to playground clumsiness, to recite her name, her age, to ask the girl for her favourite colour and if she has any pets.

The monster has no such difficulties.

'How is the weather today?'

The question is so shockingly mundane that Maia almost laughs. She wonders if it's Mrs Shepherd's doing, if her British influence has led to an excessive interest in weather-based conversation.

'Is it still as hot as it has been? Mrs Shepherd says it's been boiling the past few days.'

Maia smiles to herself as her theory is proved correct.

'Uh – yes. Yes, it has been. Still is.'

If the monster is bothered by Maia's stammering response, she gives no indication of it. Indeed, against all the odds, there is something about her that puts Maia at ease, that warms the atmosphere of the room.

Maia gets the feeling that this is something the lady of the house is well practised at – carefully steering conversation, making other people comfortable. It's more than a skill. It's a survival instinct.

'I don't get outside much,' the girl is saying now, 'and even less so during the daytime. So I'm always interested in the weather.'

Then, more self-consciously, she adds:

'I know it probably seems awfully dull to…well, to everyone else.'

'Not at all!' Maia says. Then, unthinkingly, 'Why don't you get outside?'

There is a hefty silence. Maia can practically feel the girl on the other side of the screen biting her tongue, fighting off the urge to mock the foolishness of the question. Her response, though, when it does arrive, is almost perfectly benign.

'Well, I'm rather *visible*, you see,' she says. Then, her voice dust-dry, 'I don't know if you've noticed?'

Maia lets out an undignified bark of laughter at that. Ordinarily she would flinch at such a sound coming from her mouth unbidden, even apologise for it, but the normal rules don't seem to apply here.

'So you never go outside?' she asks instead.

From the other side of the screen, there is a hum of agreement.

'I walk around the gardens here,' she says, 'but only with Mrs Shepherd, and even then, only when it starts to get dark. It's just an hour or so a day usually.'

'Where would you go if you could?'

'Honestly?'

'Yes.'

'I would run down into the village and get ice cream. And sit in the sun, eating it. It would be the perfect thing on a day like today.'

The innocent excitement of the answer makes Maia smile.

They talk a while longer after that. Half an hour, or possibly even an hour – Maia isn't quite sure. She does find, though, that the vast majority of that time is spent talking about herself. The girl behind the screen is full of questions, relentless with them.

Distantly, Maia wonders if she's genuinely interested or if this is just another screen, another way for the monster to obscure herself. It certainly works well; when Maia gets up to leave, she finds she's learnt almost nothing about her employer.

As Maia turns to the door, a glint of *something* catches her eye. There's a shimmer on the floor, a shard of refracted light. Her eyes, almost automatically, follow it up to the source.

Her heart stops.

It's not hyperbole; it really does for a moment. She feels the sudden lurching gulf of unpumped blood, the full-body shock of adrenaline.

Maia stands there absolutely still. Her eyes are wide, unblinking, as though to swallow the sight.

She can't see the whole of her. Not at all. The mirror is just barely angled where it sits, nervously, past the edge of the screen. Its reflection in this dark place is mostly a blurred mass of shadows – but, very occasionally, something stirs. An unwitting glimpse of elbow, the back of a neck. A flicker as her silhouette interrupts the candlelight.

But it's enough. Enough to render the monster of legend visible for the very first time.

When Maia finally does break the trance, it is with a quick lick of her lips – now parchment dry – and with a few words croaked out. She doesn't turn towards the screen when she speaks; her eyes stay locked in place.

'You never told me your name,' she says softly. She hopes her voice is more stable than it feels.

The monster-girl's voice is soft, even shy.

'It's Petra.'

'Petra,' Maia echoes, the name a spell on her lips. 'It was lovely to meet you, Petra.'

Her words are so quiet that she's not sure if Petra has heard them. She hopes she did.

The next time she knocks on the villa's door, the bronze knocker blazing with the Saturday afternoon heat, it doesn't swing open as it has before. Indeed, it takes several long, faltering moments before there are any signs of life at all. Just as Maia starts to worry, she hears harried, shuffling footsteps and the frantic unbolting of multiple locks.

'Good afternoon, Mrs Shepherd. Sorry I'm late.'

The housekeeper's surprise could not be more total. Her mouth hangs slack. Her fingertips tremble uncomprehendingly at her sides.

Maia smiles reflexively before she realises that the gesture is futile. Instead, she places her hand on the woman's arm and gives it a gentle squeeze, as if to confirm her own reality.

Inside the house, the gloom is even more consuming than usual. She doesn't bring any shopping today; they didn't give her a list after last time. All she carries is a bottle of wine, yanked from her grandfather's cellar and still bearing antique dust. Her arms feel oddly light, freed from the weight of a dropped pretence.

She doesn't wait for permission this time – she knows her way now, after all. She breezes across the kitchen with the ease of somebody who has been doing so their whole life. She can hear her grandfather's voice in her mind, once more: *like you own the place, my girl.*

Then she vanishes down the corridor and pretends not to see the astonishment on Mrs Shepherd's face.

She pretends not to see so many things.

She approaches Petra more boldly today. She is determined to defy the solemnity of this house, its hushed, darkened corridors, the thick mythology which coats everything here like dust.

Petra is a girl. Only a girl. And so Maia yanks out the wine cork with reckless force and pretends not to care when some splashes onto the floor. Pours herself a generous glass, leaves the second as an offering at the far end of the screen. Kicks off her shoes and sits cross-legged on her chair, like an eager child.

Then she talks. And talks some more.

It's all determinedly nonsensical – her bawdiest anecdotes, her most gossipy chatter of neighbours and school friends. Even Maia herself is only half aware of what it is, exactly, that she's saying; mostly, she just wants to fill the silence, to disrupt the terrible stillness of the air.

It works. After a few minutes, there is a flicker of movement at the edge of the screen, as Petra retrieves the glass of wine with practised stealth. She begins to chip in to the conversation, to laugh more readily. Her voice sounds, to Maia's ears, just a little less rehearsed than it did.

They carry on this way until the golden evening, as the sky melts to candlewax. The wine – a thick, syrupy dessert wine – is almost gone. They are both a little giddy, clutching their stomachs in teenage-girl laughter.

Petra slides something under the screen then, and Maia lurches down to catch it. A worn leather case, and, in it, a pack of playing cards. They're delicate with age and hold the same precious, antique appearance as everything else Petra owns. Hand-painted in rich inks, the hearts and diamonds as keen as drops of blood, kings and jokers sneering out from behind Venetian masks.

'My mother always told me that these cards belonged to Casanova himself,' Petra offers.

'Did they?'

'No,' says Petra, and they both laugh. 'But she was never one to let the truth get in the way of a good story.'

Maia moves a little closer to the screen and begins to shuffle the deck. From here, she can see Petra's shadow – angular shapes flickering out from under the screen, occasionally brushing the dark skin of Maia's knees. She studies them, trying to puzzle out hints of monstrosity like a child in the dark, but it's a pointless exercise.

She is usually deft with cards, can usually shuffle them

effortlessly, but tonight she is clumsy with wine and they slip from her hands, spilling across the floor to a chorus of giggles.

As she scrabbles them back into some semblance of order, they discuss – debate, really – what to play. Maia settles herself in more deliberately, feels where the stone of the floor has warmed under her bare legs. She lays out the cards in the slim shared space between them, beneath the gap at the bottom of the screen.

When they do start to play, it's childlike. The sort of scrappy, floor-slapping game that they really shouldn't be engaging in with cards this ancient, Casanova's or not. But when she hears a smile start to twist Petra's voice, when her quiet solemnity is finally broken as she squawks out against some perceived outrage, Maia absolutely can't bring herself to care.

'You're good at this!' Petra is forced to admit in a break between rounds. She sounds a little breathless.

Maia, mid-sip of her wine, hmms.

'My grandfather taught me to play,' she says eventually.

'He was a good teacher, then?'

Maia chuckles.

'Depends on what you mean by "good",' she says.

Petra's silence seems to invite elaboration, so she continues.

'He taught me every game going – poker and blackjack, and others that I'm not sure even have names. And he taught me how to shuffle and do magic tricks. He loved it.

'But the thing is, I would always lose. I don't mean often or most of the time – I would always, *always* lose. From when I was old enough to hold a hand of cards, until I was about fourteen or so. No matter what I did, no matter what strategy I concocted, I lost every single round, every single game. It got to a point where I really did think he could read my mind. And then he told me the truth.'

'The truth?' The very air seems to tremble.

'I never could have won.'

'Why not?'

'The games were rigged. He'd been sitting me in front of the mirror.'

'The mirror? What do you mean?'

'He could see the cards reflected. My whole hand with a single glance. All my fretting, all my desperate attempts to be secretive, all of it was pointless. I had lost from the moment I sat down. The reflection showed him everything.'

Petra laughs at this, but it's a polite laughter, an acknowledgement that the story has reached its punchline.

'And it took you that long to realise?' she says.

Maia's voice is far more solemn when she speaks again. Her words sound deliberate, emphasised, as though she's attempting to convey some vast significance.

'I never knew,' she confirms. 'I never even suspected. He hid it so well. He played dumb. But he already knew everything. He could see it all, plain as day.'

If Petra could look into Maia's eyes, she would see that they are even wider, even more watchful than usual. Their darkness holds a begging look, something that pleads with her to just *understand*.

Maia turns her head towards the mirror and traces her eyes over the barely-there image of Petra, the knowledge so forbidden that it makes her dizzy. She wishes that Petra would feel her gaze somehow, would turn to meet it. To confront it.

But, of course, she doesn't. And Maia, always so brave, finds all at once that she has become a coward. This thing, this connection between them, is spun glass, brand-new and still soft from the fire. It's so delicate, so precious, that she cannot yet bear to shatter it with such a betrayal.

Petra, for now, remains unwittingly observed. When she speaks, her blithe cheeriness makes Maia flinch.

'Well,' she says, 'you'll get no such treatment from me, I promise. I always play fair.'

Maia forces some levity into her voice. Tries to pretend that there is enough air in the room.

'I don't believe it for a second,' she says, mouth twitching in an almost-smile.

The conversation winds down after that. Maia can tell that Petra is starting to tire: her voice deepens with overuse; her quips are slower to arrive. She feels a pang of guilt that the girl might now be too worn out to enjoy her beloved night-time excursion, her only fresh air of the day. She's certain that she is a very poor consolation prize.

She gathers herself back up, shoving her feet into her shoes, not bothering to tie the laces. As she turns to go, she allows herself, with guilty hunger, a rare second look.

She doesn't even breathe. She just watches, shoulders set, dark eyes fixed.

She steps closer – just a little. She cocks her head to one side and furrows her eyebrows involuntarily, in the way she always has when faced with a curiosity, when something new digs its claws into her imagination and prepares to run away with the catch.

I know that look, her grandfather would say if he could see her now. And it was true – he had learnt to recognise it early on in Maia's childhood. It usually foretold yet another calamitous expedition – an unexpected archaeological dig of the back garden, an injured grass snake adopted and housed in a shoebox.

Most people see something new and strange, something different, and they run away screaming. Not you.

Maia smiles to herself.

No, you get closer.

She takes another step forward. Then another. Her breath shakes in the silent room. Her face is all amazement. Whatever she's looking at, it's a work of art. A scientific marvel. A wonder of the natural world.

'Goodnight, then.' Petra's voice, small in the gloom, startles Maia, although she still does not tear her gaze away, does not turn back towards the screen when she speaks.

'Goodnight, my lady.'

And she is gone.

Maia arrives early the following weekend. She expects the usual display – the door with its dozen locks, the house quietly entombed.

But today the front door is already ajar, the stale atmosphere of the corridor airing out in the summer breeze. The house looks strange like this, illuminated by the white light of the morning.

Even Petra's bedchamber is a little lighter – drapes pushed hastily aside, pale beams spearing through the gaps in the shutters. Dust particles dancing in the sunspots.

Petra wastes no time. She explains her plan almost immediately, her voice all a rush, as though she's afraid she'll lose her nerve.

'I thought – if you *want* to – we could do away with this today? The screen, I mean.'

Maia makes a slight, strangled noise at the very back of her throat. She hopes the sound was too small to carry to Petra's ears.

She thinks this morning could not take a more surprising turn. She's wrong.

'You still can't look at me, of course,' Petra continues. 'But I thought – well, I know it seems odd, but I thought you could wear this?'

It takes Maia a minute to puzzle out what exactly it is that Petra slides towards her underneath the screen, to discern some sense out of the bundle of white cotton.

A blindfold.

Petra has given her a blindfold.

The silence between them is long and expectant. Maia fights her usual urge to fill it pointlessly, to shatter this strange tension with one of the half-dozen cheap innuendos that the blindfold seems to invite. But this moment is too important. Too important to ruin.

'Of course, I could just…look at you,' Maia offers, finally.

'Nice try,' says Petra.

Maia can hear the wry smile in her voice; she wonders if that's real, or if it is just another expert construction. One of Petra's endless hiding places.

Maia fumbles the supple fabric in her hands, trying to figure out the best way to tie it. Suddenly, this all seems so terribly real that her hands go bloodless.

'How shall we do this?' she asks. 'I could turn around, if you like, and you can check it's all tied on – or you could tie it, if you prefer?'

'I trust you,' Petra says.

She says it so comfortably, so easily, that it devastates Maia. *You shouldn't*, she wants to say.

'OK,' she replies instead, with a shaky breath. She wishes she was braver, more honest. More worthy of this, whatever it is.

She lifts the fabric to cover her eyes. She ties it snug and tight, so that there is not even the slightest trickle of light at the edges of her vision. Then she knots it, feels the loose tendrils of excess fabric trailing down her neck. She breathes the words again: 'OK, then.'

Slowly, with an almost ceremonial significance, she rises from where she had been kneeling on the floor. Brushes the creases from her dress with trembling hands.

Maia steps forward with her hands outstretched in front of her, feeling through the empty space. A particularly surreal game of blind man's bluff.

One step, two, and then she meets the wall of the screen in front of her, feels her way to the edge and steps past it. Right into the monster's lair.

Petra doesn't notice the surety of Maia's steps, the ease with which she skirts around a jutting table edge. The way she orientates herself so naturally in the shadowed space with something that could almost be called familiarity.

It starts softly, as life-altering things often do. Maia does not rush or grab; she simply waits, offering her hand.

Petra takes it. Her own hand is feather-light, a hollow-boned creature ready to fly at the first sign of trouble. It's not the difference which startles Maia, but the familiarity – how very human this feels. The warmth of the skin, the callouses here and there. She runs her thumb along a fingernail and finds it jagged, bitten to the quick.

This makes her smile. She, too, is a nail-biter.

She lifts the hand and kisses it, the skin of the knuckles

dry under her lips. There is something ancient, something chivalric about the gesture that suits Maia well.

'Your hands are so warm,' she says, because there is nothing else to say.

'Mm,' Petra says. Her voice is removed somehow. It sounds much further than an arm's length away. 'I'm not actually cold-blooded, you know, it's—'

Her words hitch for a second. Maia is running her fingertips up and down Petra's forearm now, the barest ghost of a touch. Petra pushes on, her voice a little strangled.

'It's a common misconception,' she breathes at last.

'Fascinating,' Maia says. Her voice is laced with irony, but the sentiment is genuine.

When she reaches out to Petra again, her touch is scientific. She trembles her hands over the odd angles of her joints, presses her thumbs into the uneven hollows of her collarbones. She maps it all out with her fingertips – the great smooth plains of unaffected skin, and the other places, where her differences are more apparent.

There are patches of scar tissue, glossy and soft to the touch, and bony, calcified contortions, and other textures, strangenesses that she can neither recognise nor name.

Every time Petra flinches away, Maia stops in her tracks, lifts her hands and simply waits.

Petra always reaches out again, always guides Maia's hands back up into her own. Maia can feel the tension in her, the nervous tautness of her muscles just beneath the skin. She must be terrified. Everything in her is telling her to flee. And yet she persists, anchors herself to the floor, holds her head high and proud as Maia traces the outline of her jaw, measures the distance to her lips in the span of her fingers.

There is such a peculiar brand of courage in Petra's shallow breaths, her determined stillness. There is such great strength in breaking the habit of a lifetime, forgetting the lessons long since beaten into her, and allowing somebody to get close.

It's remarkable. She is remarkable.

'That's enough,' Petra says suddenly, and Maia's hands are gone.

'Are you alright? Did I—'

'I'm fine.' Petra's voice is hasty. 'I just can't let this go on any longer.'

'Why not?'

'Because it isn't fair to you.'

'*Fair* to me?'

'It's not...' Petra fumbles for the words. 'It's not honest. I'm – I feel as if I'm taking advantage.'

Maia's stomach jolts in recognition. How startling it is to hear her own thoughts reflected back at her so precisely.

'If you knew,' Petra continues desperately. 'If you could see me exactly as I am, you wouldn't be here. You wouldn't want to touch me. It's not right, Maia. You don't know what it is you're doing—'

'I know more than you think.' Maia's voice is a snap in the dark.

This is the closest they've come to a real fight, she realises. There is a strange, giddy victory in it, in the normality of it.

Maia steadies herself. Tries again.

'You're underestimating me,' she says. 'Insulting me, really. You're treating me like I'm a girl in a fairy tale, tricked by the wicked monster.'

'Aren't you?'

'*No*, Petra. I'm real. So are you, for that matter. Just as much of a person as I am.'

Petra's laugh is as dark and as bitter as ash. It sounds entirely wrong for her, discordant with the usual softness of her voice.

'You wouldn't say that if you could *see*—'

'Yes, I would.'

Maia's voice brings everything to a dead stop.

'You can't know that.'

'But I do.' It is Maia who sounds young now, her voice desperately quiet. But it holds a certainty, and a fear, which shakes Petra. This is a confession.

Petra says nothing. For the first time since they began this game, or even since they met, Maia feels the full weight of her disadvantage. She wishes she could see Petra's face.

She's poised for further explanation – ready to instruct Petra more specifically, to reveal the mirror, the cheap gambler's trick of it.

In the end, she doesn't need to. Petra is clever, a brilliance sharpened by a lifetime of self-protection, and so it takes just one swift patrol of her footsteps around the room before she reaches the truth.

Maia stays stone still. Tries not to flinch at the clattering groan of the screen as Petra pushes it aside, or the moment of faltering silence that follows.

She waits, gives Petra time. Then she lifts her blindfold, pressing her eyes tightly shut as she does so. Even though the gesture is pointless, it seems, somehow, to be the only act of decency she has left. The only choice she can offer Petra now.

'Open your eyes.'

Maia does. She is dazzled by the light for a second, by its liquid quality as it streams in far above her. Then she turns around in a single movement, the flagstones smooth and yielding under her feet.

She looks into the corner, to the spot where she knows the mirror – the damningly angled mirror – will be waiting.

'I'm sorry,' she says to Petra's reflection. 'I should have told you sooner. I didn't know how.'

'How long?' Petra asks. 'How long has it been like this?'

'Since our first meeting.' It is the heaviest confession Maia has yet made.

Petra approaches her then. Maia does not move to face her, just watches the girl's reflection become clearer, more real by the second. When Petra reaches her, she tugs lightly on Maia's shoulder, entreating her to turn around.

Maia looks into Petra's eyes. She has never seen them before today. She makes a conscious effort to commit their colour to memory in case she is never allowed to look at them again. In case Petra banishes her now, turns her out into the unforgiving light.

She doesn't. She presses closer, so that Maia can feel the warmth of her. Skates one hand, with absolute caution, over the skin of Maia's elbow, inviting her in.

Their story begins, and ends, in the tradition of all good fairy tales. With a kiss.

On another day, in another summer, Maia races through the village square.

You wouldn't notice her if you saw her – at least, not particularly. Curly dark hair and a hurried flash of a grin. Just another pretty girl in a rush. Easily lost in the summer-holiday crowds.

She holds an ice-cream cone in each hand, and they're melting rapidly in the midday sun. She lifts her thumb to her lips, makes a frantic attempt to lick up the melted trail. In doing so, she nearly drops the other cone, and swears to herself under her breath.

At the fountain, in the heart of the square, she stops. She *beams*, an expression that reduces her previous smile to nothingness, to a mere shadow.

She has spotted her companion.

They sit side by side, perched on the edge of the fountain, Maia and this other girl. They laugh and squabble and adorn each other's noses with ice cream.

At one point, the other girl removes her shoes, dipping her toes softly in the water. Beside her, Maia climbs up, performs an outsized tightrope walk along the fountain's edge, dissolving into laughter when she nearly falls in.

Maia is animated, her arms a constant blur, but her companion's silhouette is far more shuttered. Even now, her frame is careful, watchful. She glances around every few moments. She can never stay for long.

Sometimes, if you look closely, you'll snatch a glimpse of her – between passing crowds, or over Maia's shoulder. You will see something astonishing, a sheer impossibility that sets your heart racing.

If you're very curious, you might even push forward, seek out a second look. But she's always gone by then. There's never any sign of her, no evidence left behind of the strange thing you thought you saw.

Perhaps it was only a trick of the light.

The Body

Afterwards, I felt nothing at all.

If I hadn't still been wearing my hospital gown, there would have been no indication that any procedure had taken place. I was in no pain.

There was just this gap, an absence; a great blank gulf where sensation used to be.

My mouth was thickly encased with the alien taste of absolutely nothing. A new-car taste, all sealed, sterile air. It didn't even taste like water, which still always tastes of *something* – chalk or chemicals or the rusty tap, or even the merest hint of your own blood. It was just this hollowness, stark against my factory-fresh taste buds.

Other things began to register. The small things first. The nudging toothache I had been steadfastly ignoring for two weeks was gone. The old smatterings of bruises had been lifted from my shins, leaving them pristine. The hangnail on my right thumb was healed and whole again.

I took an inventory of all this trivia before I allowed myself to process the rest of it. The full enormity of the transformation. There was a looseness, an ease to my body. A startling absence of spasticity, of the little involuntary spasms that usually made themselves known around my knees and ankles.

There was an odd new proximity between my brain and my limbs, commands twitching themselves into existence almost before I had thought them. It was that quick. There was no fight now, no wrangling of my muscles into submission. My toes, beneath the covers, flexed and danced with ease. My body was doing exactly what bodies are supposed to do.

I had expected a sweeping elation, maybe a rush of grief and tears. I hadn't expected the dry, brittle anger that suddenly consumed me. *Has it always been this easy for everyone else?*

I stood up, swung my legs out of bed. There was something slightly unnerving about the way my feet connected so certainly with the floor, a sharp, decisive right angle of ankle and sole. The cool smoothness of the linoleum against my heels was new and strangely overwhelming.

I bounced a little, up-down, testing the parameters. A small jump next, the briefest spell of air between myself and the ground. This brand-new, miraculous gravity, of this brand-new, miraculous body. I might as well have been taking flight.

I remembered what Dr Arnold had told me when he first showed me the new body, laid out on its chrome table.

It had been built in my image, more or less. My measurements, but slimmed down, streamlined. My skin tone, but clear, and closed, and shining.

The resemblance was not as startling as I had expected. It's funny how one's flaws add up. And, of course, the new body lacked my tightness – had none of my rigidity in the tiny muscles beneath the face. That made a difference.

Dr Arnold had given me his best used-car-salesman smile and said, all lazy self-assurance, 'I think you'll be satisfied.'

I had been. Very satisfied. Enough to sign the paperwork right then and there.

'Is it reversible?' I had asked, watching the ink of my signature congeal.

'No,' he had said.

I had answered, 'Good.'

As soon as I was up and walking, I asked to see my old body.

They were reluctant at first. They wouldn't let me leave my room until I had passed a neurological examination, until they were sure I wasn't suffering any side effects.

When they finally did lead me to it, it was a long

journey. Miles of twisting back corridors, then down three floors in an echoey service lift to the clinic basement. Then more corridors, bare and unwelcoming, starkly lit by long strips of fluorescent lights overhead.

Down there, it smelt of hospitals – which was odd, because none of the rest of this place did.

They showed me into a small, windowless room and left me alone. It was cold inside; the walls and ceiling were all stark white tiles, the floor a worn vinyl which sloped inwards towards a small, central drain.

I had expected the body to be laid out – if not in a plush hospital bed like my own, then at least on a metal table – but instead it was on the floor, a crumpled heap in the farthest corner. It was naked.

Its back was to me, so I couldn't see the face, couldn't see any of those unsavoury, difficult details.

Much later, I would learn that they placed it this way on purpose. That it was a strategic decision, intended to cushion the initial shock of that first glance for the few who chose to look. This made me laugh when I heard it, because nothing in the world could ever possibly have prepared me for the sight of it, once I stepped closer. For the ugliness of it.

Because it *was* ugly – that was my overwhelming impression, even from a distance. The pallor of its flesh was ugly, all of the places where it bulged and sagged as it pressed into the floor.

It was shockingly real. A bare horror, the naked back

with its patches of acne and long-forgotten sunburn, the bunched-up cellulite.

When I could finally bring myself to touch it, which took some time, the first thing I did was run my fingertips down the brazen ridge of the spine, feeling my way through all the uneven notches. I found my target, the soft, bulging spot where it started to distort, and I pressed my fingertips into it as hard as I possibly could, watching the flesh blanch and the bruises start to form. I tried to remember the specificity of that pain, how the vulnerable, exposed cord would send shockwaves through me if it was even nudged. I savoured the memory. Pressed harder.

It filled me with strength. I grabbed the thing more decisively by the shoulders, pulling it over towards me. This was harder than I'd imagined; it was like the body itself was resisting me.

As it finally shifted, I was hit by the smell of it. It wasn't the scent of a corpse; the body wasn't dead, after all, just unoccupied. It smelt warm, human. Sweat-damp skin and unwashed hair and the merest traces of my own perfume. The familiarity of it, the intense intimacy, made me gag uncontrollably – great, wrenching spasms – until I was spitting thin bile into the drain behind me.

That's the thing they don't tell you about the body. It's offensive on a *personal* level.

I redoubled my efforts. I tried to take comfort in the new-found strength of my arms, the smoothness of their mobility. I tried not to breathe too deeply.

Finally, I felt the body give way and roll to face me. I looked down and saw my own eyes blinking back up at me.

There was something embarrassing about seeing my own face from this angle, from above. It felt a little like unexpectedly hearing a snatch of your voice on a tape recording, too loud and too deep and altogether wrong. Thinking, *Dear god, have I really been going around in the world this way? Have they really been letting me?*

I saw that my eyes weren't as dark as I had thought, and that the bridge of my nose was much wider. I had always thought that the appearance of my face, at least, was unaffected, that my impairment wasn't visible in *that* way. But from the outside, a lopsidedness was undeniable; the slow, thick smile, the one eye that lagged slightly behind the other.

I could see the muscles underneath the flesh still pulled taut, the rigid woodenness of the limbs and the way the hands postured into fists instinctively – the brain still firing off its spastic signals, even after everything else was emptied out. There was something stubborn about it, something determined.

If it hadn't been so hideous, I might almost have admired it.

As it was, I just stared at it, at this thing that had once been me. I looked at the feet which still, even now, turned uselessly inwards, the knees that bumped together with a hollow knock as the body's weight shifted. I looked at the toes, thick with the calluses of misuse, the hands cracked dry, the slightest smudges of ink on the fingertips of the left hand. The chest that still, on autopilot, rose and fell in steady breaths.

I wanted to set it on fire. To punch it as hard as I possibly could. To tear out its eyes and methodically yank out its teeth, one at a time.

They had warned me about these feelings, so-called 'upwellings of violent impulse'. It was a common side effect, apparently. I hadn't listened to them. I hadn't even really believed them.

I was not, I had thought, a violent person. Nobody had ever accused me of being particularly hateful or vitriolic. I found it hard to imagine myself seized by destructive urges, not in any serious way.

I hadn't known then the effect that the body would have on me. I was naïve. I didn't know that it would hit me somewhere deep, somewhere primal.

I didn't know how ugly I would be from the outside.

I had chosen to dispose of the body myself.

We had had a meeting about it at the clinic, my whole care team sitting around a conference table, wearing thoughtful, attentive expressions. The room had been quiet, almost uncomfortably so, but if I listened carefully, I could just about hear the muffled chants of the protesters outside. It was a distant, unreal sound. Nobody but me seemed to notice it, and even I found that it faded quickly into background noise.

The doctors had laid everything out in front of me in a glossy brochure. *Your Options.* I remember flicking through it, pressing my fingertips into the sharp edges of each page. It was proper, quality paper. Good and thick.

'Most people choose to dispose of the surplus body after the procedure,' said the nurse next to me. 'In that case, it's treated essentially as medical waste. We offer a cremation service for a small additional fee.'

I nodded wordlessly.

Dr Arnold chipped in then. 'Around ninety per cent of our patients opt for that. We recommend it, really. Our research suggests it provides – well, a clean break, as it were. There are psychological benefits.'

'If you have financial concerns,' added the assistant surgeon, 'you can also surrender the body to the clinic for experimentation. That would actually offer you a slight rebate on your procedure fee—'

'And we really value that kind of contribution,' Dr Arnold added hastily. 'It helps us develop and refine the procedure, make it safer for future patients. Invaluable, really.'

I was quiet for a while. I looked again at the brochure, the endless pages of pristine images and user-friendly fonts. There was a surreal sense of vagueness about the whole thing. None of the images seemed to relate to anything else. The page on *Permanent Disposal* was dominated by a smiling woman wearing a stripy dress and playing building blocks with a toddler. In *Long-Term Maintenance*, an old man walked a Border collie.

'What about the other ten per cent?' I asked. 'What do they choose?'

Dr Arnold looked a little startled. Shuffled in his seat.

'Well, there are long-term care facilities,' he said slowly. 'They maintain the surplus body for you, keep it hydrated, that sort of thing. So that you can...visit it, and things.'

From his tone, it was clear this wasn't a choice he supported, or even understood. To me, too, it seemed perverse. To treat the body like a conscious thing and not just instincts bouncing around a hollow interior. To fuss over it.

'Of course, there are some very substantial costs associated with that. Or...'

He paused. It was unusual for him to hesitate. My eyes darted up to him.

'Or you can retain the surplus body. That is, you can sign a waiver and bring it home with you. That's a cost-neutral option.'

I had heard of this. It was the notorious choice, the stuff of horror stories and sensationalised slush in cheap magazines. There were all sorts of rumours about the things people did with their old bodies.

I'm still not sure why I chose it.

I had been so callous, so cavalier up to that point; I was ready to cast my body aside, to launch head first into the procedure.

I suppose I had some half-formed idea that this would offer me a very particular kind of closure – to see to the body myself. To say goodbye to it for good.

And, if I'm honest, I baulked a little at the sheer permanence of it, my old bones turned to ash. The prospect had curdled at the pit of my stomach.

'I'll do that,' I said quickly. 'I'll sign the waiver. I'll keep my body – I mean, my surplus body.'

There was silence in the room. It was only a few seconds, maybe not even that, but it was there – a rare falter, a disruption to the perfect slickness of this place.

Dr Arnold looked at me, still leaning back in his chair. For a moment, I thought I saw some flicker of worry, even of anger, on his face – but as he answered me, it smoothed over, implacable as ever. Perhaps I had imagined it.

'Of course,' he said. 'Legal will send the paperwork over to you this week.'

I had made the decision so quickly, so unthinkingly, that only as they all filed out of the room did I realise I had no idea what I would actually do with the body when I had it.

Nobody ever thinks about the physicality of a body, the weight of it. Five and a half feet of conspicuous flesh.

At first I had imagined shutting it quietly away somewhere. In my attic, maybe, or a locked cupboard beneath the stairs.

But when I was confronted with it, still warm and blinking, when I, fresh out of the clinic, dragged it through my front door in the half-light of morning, such plans felt impossibly naïve.

So, in the end, I did what came most naturally. I buried it.

It took me most of the day to dig the grave. The earth in my back garden was hard and dry and almost deliberately awkward. I could feel the brand-new bones in my wrist jolting as the shovel tip bounced harmlessly against the crust of the ground.

When the cavity did start to emerge, it was rather pathetic. A crumbled, noncommittal thing, all uncertain edges. I had wanted it six feet deep, but this barely scraped four.

I tried to treat the whole enterprise as a test drive of my new body. I immersed myself in the wonder of straight legs and flat feet, of using my arms freely without having to lean. Moving without pain. Strength, the likes of which I had only ever been able to imagine.

I crawled out of the grave. The blisters on my hands had long since burst and were now weeping openly. I felt a sweeping resentment that my new skin, so pristine, was already damaged.

Closing up the grave was easier than digging it had been. The body put up only the most minimal resistance, a token scrabbling, nothing more. It was easy to subdue, especially with the aid of strategically placed shovelfuls of dirt.

I covered the face first. That made everything else much more straightforward.

I packed it all in as tightly as I could, enclosing the awkward angles of the joints, everything firm and snug so that the wriggling would stop. When I had piled all the loose dirt back on, I smoothed it over into a neat mound.

It was a little unfortunate, this big dark stain on the lawn. I thought, *Maybe I could plant flowers.*

When it was done, I went out. It felt odd to step out of the front door with no wheelchair, no bag of medications, none of the paraphernalia I was so used to. I tottered awkwardly down my wheelchair ramp and made a mental note to remove it.

I walked down the street, adjusting myself to the new angle of the world.

In the park, a big group from the residential home were collecting signatures for a petition. I watched them, a cluttered crowd of wheelchairs and motorised scooters. They didn't smile at me; there was no look of recognition. It took me a second to remember that I wasn't one of them anymore, that they saw nothing of themselves in me.

I was just another gawker now.

I crossed the park to sign. It was only halfway through writing my name that I realised that I held the pen in my right hand, that my new body was not left-handed as my old one had been.

That had been fixed, with everything else.

When I came home, the first thing I did was open my back door to check on the grave.

It was empty.

It gaped stupidly, gasping its shock into the evening air. Beside it, the rumpled duvet of freshly turned dirt, thrown frantically aside.

I tried not to panic. The thing could hardly have gone far. It could barely walk even when it was properly alive.

The air was still cold, and a low, hesitant fog had settled with the dusk. I trudged across the fields behind the house, trampling easily over the stubble of dead crops, the built-up debris of bricks and rocks and littered plastic bags.

I found the body within half an hour. It had travelled a pathetic distance, not even a mile. It bore thick black crescents of grave dirt beneath its fingernails, a painted beard of spat-out mud across its chin. It was crawling, its knees bloody as they scraped helplessly against the hard troughs of dirt, the sharp, hidden stones lodged within.

I looked at it and remembered my first surgery, when I was seven, when the casts on both my legs had forced me back to crawling. I remembered my knees dragging on the carpets until they bled.

The crawl of my old body was identical still. Those few months lived on in my muscle memory, had pervaded my biology.

I looked down at my new knees, pristine and soft. Nothing bad had ever happened to this body. No surgeon had ever cut open these legs, held these muscles in their gloved hands. It wasn't *this* blood that still stained the carpets of my childhood home.

How strange, to be brand-new again. To live in a body that had never been touched.

When I reached it, the body collapsed in a naked heap at my feet. I nudged it with my toe, just once, prising it up from the ground like roadkill. For some reason, I found I couldn't resist the urge.

Then I hauled it over my shoulder, carried it home and threw it back into the waiting grave.

I covered it with reckless shovelfuls of dirt, smoothed over the mound of earth, sealing it up, closing off the air. I felt sure that all was now resolved, that this last flare of defiance had been quelled.

I went to bed. I dreamt of purple plaster casts, sweat-itching, scrawled over with Sharpie pen. The scrape of carpet on my knees.

When I woke, the grave was empty once more.

We continued in this way for weeks. I became ever more creative in my burials, obsessing over containers, weights, bicycle chains, locks, wet cement; sketching new grave designs like a woman possessed. I thought of nothing but ways to be rid of my body for good.

After the first fortnight of burials, I grabbed a kitchen knife – still warm and damp on the draining board – and punctured the body's neck, the hot, throbbing hub of the artery.

I hoped to drain the body of blood, to bury it pale and slack and unresisting. To render it lifeless and finally know peace.

But the body wouldn't bleed.

The smallest spurt, perhaps, just enough to slick my fingertips, but it would stop the same moment. No matter how deep, the cut would congeal and clot. When I tried to hold it open, the would would heal around my hands, swallowing me whole.

The body wore a victorious look, an almost-smile, a baring of teeth. It made me hate it even more. This body. Its hideousness. Its stubborn, stubborn blood.

Once, in a fury of primitive instinct, I tried to set it on fire.

It wouldn't light, of course. It turned to driftwood and smouldered damply. The ends of its hair were slightly singed, but that was the extent of the damage.

Through the dull air, the body just blinked at me, as if to say, *Really?*

The name plate beside his door was brushed chrome, with the letters embossed on it in black. *Dr G. Arnold.* The font was pleasingly minimalistic.

I hadn't been here since the procedure. I had forgotten just how pristine this whole place was, all tinted glass and silky-smooth metal and furniture that looked as if nobody had ever touched it. The staff smiled serenely, and vast canvases of generic scientific imagery lined the waiting room, microscopic photography of neurons and nano-particles. Opposite me, a full-body MRI was splayed out across the wall.

They sent me in. Dr Arnold smiled when he saw me – that perfectly symmetrical smile of his.

'It's so lovely to see you again,' he said, 'although I do wish it could be under happier circumstances.'

I studied his face. I remembered that I had found his perfection attractive before, but there was something a little unsettling about it now.

He had the uniformity, the general quality of smoothness, which is distinctive to those who have undergone the procedure. His skin, like mine, was featureless – with no pores or scars or freckles or spots or marks of any kind – untouched by the world, carrying an airbrushed, artificial sheen.

It was impossible to guess at his age, or what sort of life he had lived, or to access any interior information about him at all. His body was a wall, a great blank barrier. The overwhelming impression was one of handsome vagueness.

I told him about the problems I had been having – about my efforts to destroy my old body. I found myself sanding off the edges as I spoke, leaving the most damning details unsaid, letting them hover in the potential space of implication.

Still, I listed everything I had tried in the barest, most clinical language I could muster. Burial. Bleeding. Burning.

He listened, humming respectfully at the appropriate times. Sitting there in his white coat, a look of perfect concern stitched on his face, I thought he could have been a stock photo. *Sympathetic doctor.*

'This does sometimes happen,' he said, once I had finally finished. 'Very rarely – but sometimes. The procedure just doesn't take. Like rejecting an organ.'

Distantly, I wondered why this hadn't been mentioned in any of the brochures. It seemed a rather glaring oversight.

Dr Arnold was unapologetic, though. He continued, his voice still unreachably calm. 'I must admit, the level of resistance you describe does seem unusually robust.'

For half a second, his expression shifted. It seemed almost as though something real and uncompromising might finally break the surface tension of his body's docility. I leant forward, keen to see how fear or anger, or some other incompatible ugliness, would register on his artificial features.

But when he spoke, his voice was as controlled as ever.

'In cases like yours, there tends to be an element of... well, a reluctance to let go. That uncertainty is what feeds the surplus body, what keeps it alive.'

He paused. Perhaps he was wrestling with himself, but it was impossible to tell.

'Look, if you're really serious about this, the only way forward is to embrace your new life, once and for all. You have to really *choose* it, make a definitive choice.'

'I am,' I said. 'I'm trying.'

His gaze was shrewd. He could see right to the very core of me. It made me feel at a disadvantage; I understood nothing of him.

'Are you?'

A *definitive choice*. That, I could do.

I dressed the old body quickly and carelessly. A charity shop fleece, stained tracksuit bottoms. Loose, unsentimental clothing, easy to put on it without too much close contact. Clothes I wasn't afraid to lose.

I led the body to my car by the hand. Surprisingly, it didn't resist me. I eased it into the backseat like a child, leaning over to plug its seatbelt when it fumbled numbly through the half-remembered act.

Before we left, I collected my wheelchair from the garage. It was cold and dusty, its tyres spongy with recent neglect – after all, I had had no need of it since the procedure – but it would do well enough for today's purpose. I packed it into the boot.

It was strange to drive like this, with just my hands, while my legs, now perfectly capable, sat there redundant.

I would have to retake my test, I supposed, have my car's adaptations reversed. So many things I hadn't thought about.

I watched the body in the rear-view mirror. It was slouched against the window, cheek contorted by the glass, pupils sliding back and forth as they chased passing cars.

I couldn't believe how absolutely idiotic it looked, how helpless. I wondered if that was a result of its present emptiness, or – far more horrifying – if that was just the way I had always looked, before. The way the world had seen me.

I tore my eyes away from the mirror. When we arrived, I dropped the body into the wheelchair a little more abruptly than was strictly necessary.

I balanced a large pair of sunglasses on its nose in a half-hearted effort to disguise our uncanny resemblance. As we set off, I mentally ran through my excuses, outlandish even to my own ears. *My disabled sister. I take care of her. My disabled twin.*

It all proved unnecessary anyway. It was a grey, unextraordinary day, and there were hardly any people on the promenade. Those that were there didn't seem capable of noticing that the body in the wheelchair was my doppelgänger. They barely even glanced at it.

We walked a long way. To the right of us, a sheer concrete drop, all man-made in harsh, artificial right angles. The sea frothed and bayed against it, entirely uninviting.

We went even further, to the place where the promenade gave way to a more precarious sea-wall path. The wind was much harsher here, peppered by a light spit of rain. The body's jumper had hitched up awkwardly, and I could see the pale skin of its forearm, wet with sea spittle, thickened by goosebumps.

I felt an impulse to pull the sleeve down, before realising that such a thing would be ridiculous.

We had reached a good, quiet spot by then. Comfortably empty of people. The gentle curve of the sea wall allowed us to remain more or less out of view. I stayed dead still for a moment, listening, but could hear no sign of anyone approaching.

The body was unusually passive. Its head had lolled forward, chin jutting into its chest, sunglasses sliding forward on its nose, but it didn't move to correct itself. It was slumped slightly in its seat, arms hanging low and knocking against the spokes of the wheelchair. I could see a white band of exposed flesh at the waist where I hadn't pulled the trousers up properly. It didn't try to cover itself. It stayed absolutely still.

It seemed to me that the body knew what was coming now, knew what I had brought it here for. Perhaps it was trying to save itself – to say: *You don't have to do this. I won't cause any more fuss. I'll be good. I'll be good.*

Or perhaps its pliancy was just a last jab, a final effort to spite me. Perhaps it was playing helpless, trying to make me feel guilty.

If so, it was wildly overestimating my moral character.

I eased the wheelchair forward, right to the edge of the

path, until I could see the front wheels peeking out above the open air and frothing sea; until I could feel the tell-tale tug, the weight making its inevitable journey downward. Gravity doing its work.

Then, with very little ceremony, I tipped the chair forward as steeply as I possibly could.

The body plummeted. Its feet had caught under the footplate somehow, so it ended up falling head first. It nearly took the chair, and me, with it, but I managed to pull myself back just in time.

It tumbled down, bones smacking dully against the concrete wall as it went, head knocked back with a sudden jerk and a half-imagined flash of red.

It took a long time to sink. This was my fault. I hadn't weighted it in any way; I hadn't even thought to. Naïvely, I had pictured a Hollywood moment – a cinematic sinking of flesh, slow but undeniable. The body disappearing for good, swallowed by the depths.

If I had used my common sense, I would have realised that I had always floated in that body, had always bobbed quite happily, a fleck of sea foam, on the frothing top layer of the water. More than that, I had been a strong swimmer. And my body remembered.

I watched it flail, watched its arms fight the current. After some effort, it managed to roll onto its back. I watched it coerce its rigid legs into a feeble sort of kick, working off its borrowed trainers and letting them sink. Then I listened as it tried, without any meaningful success, to calm its breathing, to gain some command over the hyperventilation of cold-water shock.

It was fascinating to watch this survival instinct in action. To see how deeply it ran, how much the body wanted to live.

Still, it was with some relief that I saw its instincts start to falter. I didn't know what I would do if the body had simply stayed afloat like that, staring at me. Or, worse, if we had been spotted, if I had been forced to explain this scene to an outsider.

The waves were rough against the sea wall. More and more often, the body's half-voluntary breaths would coincide with the great white crash of the enraged ocean. I could hear its lungs filling up, the ugly plughole gurgle as they became oversaturated.

This was a losing battle. Three of the body's four limbs were injured, jutting from the water at strange angles like exposed bones. Its lips and tongue were quite blue. Its clothes billowed and swelled as the water tangled them. Beside its head, the merest seep of pink, where blood was still managing to leak, apparently faster than the body could clot it.

It was a painful watch, even for me. I stepped back, easing myself onto the seat of my wheelchair, where I stayed, perched. I waited there for the next twenty minutes or so, getting up to check on the body periodically. After five minutes, it had lost consciousness and was being buffeted unresistingly against the sea wall. After ten, it was half submerged, appearing only very occasionally as a bubble of fabric or a neat, pale row of toes breaking the surface.

After fifteen minutes, there was no sign of it at all. It had disappeared totally from view. I waited five more minutes, just to be sure, to confirm what, really, I already knew.

The body was gone.

I used the wheelchair to get back to my car. I thought this would invite less concern than pushing it empty or abandoning it on the path.

It wasn't as easy as I had thought it would be. I had no instinct for it; my muscle memory had been wiped clean. I didn't know which way to turn, where to centre my weight. My arm muscles felt too liquid, my hands off-puttingly soft against the cold metal. There was a fraudulent sensation to the tucked-away power of my legs. They rested uneasily against the footplate, artificially still.

It unmoored me a little, to realise that this part of me was gone.

I made it back to the car, leaping out of the chair and throwing it into the boot. My speed and perfect gait earned me some confused glances from the few remaining stragglers across the car park, but I couldn't bring myself to worry about it anymore. The last few hours had punctured me. I wanted to be at home.

I felt a strange, nervous thrill as I drove away. It was the feeling of having forgotten something, or perhaps just of having left something behind. I felt too light. I was untethered, cut free, plummeting endlessly upwards into an ever-thinner atmosphere. There was nobody left to catch me.

In Dr Arnold's waiting room, I was confident. I hummed with pride. I had not seen the body in over a week. It had not come back to life, not crawled back to me like some monstrous sea creature from the depths of the ocean.

I had made the *definitive choice*. I had adjusted. I had embraced my new body in all its ease.

The only other patient was a little girl with her mother. I guessed that she was perhaps six years old. She was decked out in pink, all frills, her trainers a dazzle of sequins.

She had glasses, proper little-girl glasses, goggleish and wrapped tight around her ears. And when she removed her cardigan, I saw she wore a back brace.

It was pink too, naturally. Hard, moulded plastic with a blurry design of cartoon flowers. The material was familiar to me. I had worn leg splints much the same. Or, I supposed, my old body had. Not me. Not anymore.

She skipped around the waiting room, playing hopscotch on an imaginary grid. She grinned at me, her teeth splayed and gappy.

I wondered what her disposal plan was after the procedure. I wondered if the small body which now stood smiling at me would be in the ninety per cent destroyed as medical waste. I thought of her, bagged and burnt, her milk teeth crumbling to ash and her curved spine dissolving into non-existence.

I felt a desperate urge to grab her by the shoulders then. To shake her until those baby teeth rattled, to scream, *You don't need to do this.* To scream, *Please, please, don't.*

But, of course, I didn't.

'Alayah?'

The little girl took her mother's hand, vanished into the open door of the consultation room. Dr Arnold offered her a uniform smile, exposing his rows of perfect teeth.

Their appointment would not be a long one; introductory sessions never were. It was only fifteen minutes or so before Dr Arnold stepped out again, calling my name.

I didn't hear him, of course. I was already gone by then.

When I got home, the old body stood dripping in my living room. I was not surprised to see it, but the sight still hit me hard, the full, crushing force of inevitability.

Stood might be an exaggeration, anyway. The limited capability it had once had for standing was all but gone now, snatched by the wild waves and the cement sea wall and *me.*

Its legs were all crooked and at wrong angles, one knee bent back, the opposite hip dislocated, snapped out of joint. It hunched over the carpet, the one unscathed arm propped forward to hold its shipwrecked weight, the other guarded close against its chest.

One of its teeth was missing, and there was a small graze at its hairline, which looked as though it had recently been bloody but was already healing up in that strange, supernatural way. Its neck, too, was crooked. Just slightly. Enough to make it look disapproving as it stared me down.

I didn't recognise the noise I made when I first saw it there. Something lower, uglier than a scream; an involuntary spasm of absolute frustration. Not a cry for help exactly, because it was drenched in a consuming knowledge that there was no help. Not for me. Not for this.

The body lurched towards me, pushing itself forward on its good arm, forcing its mangled one into an outstretched reach. I watched the seawater drip from its clothes and soak into the carpet. I watched its rock-torn teeth chatter uncontrollably.

Then, very slowly, it began an upwards shift. It was so gradual that I didn't understand what I was seeing at first, thought it was just another terrifying contortion of damaged flesh. It was forcing itself upwards, knocking its joints back into place with locked-shut fists, forcing the bones and muscles into place by hand.

Each individual tendon strained under the skin of the feet as it lifted onto tiptoe, made itself taller; its spine was rippling with the effort and yet it never stopped, not once, until it had put itself back together again, standing tight and tall in all its spastic glory: feet lifted, jaw tipping up, hands tightly clenched even now.

Then it let out a yell. A wild, animal yell into the closed-off sky.

It struck me that the sound was not altogether dissimilar to my horrified shout a minute ago, although the body's voice was uglier by far even than that. It held all the qualities I had always so hated about my own voice: the muscular tightness, the huskiness of uncertain hearing.

It did something to me, to hear that sound again. It was a specific, a precise pain.

I slapped the body hard across the face, my hand ringing.

Its head jerked to the side, its neck flexing suddenly. It stayed there for a second, looking away from me, frozen. Then it turned back, studying me with guileless eyes, oblivious to the rapidly reddening handprint across its cheek.

I hit it again. Then a few times more. Made a game of it, seeing how long it took the body to set itself to rights each time, seeing if an instinctive flinch would ever betray its vacant apathy.

I thought, perhaps, it might fight back. That those furious survival instincts might kick in once more, that it might block me, hit me, throw me aside. I anticipated it so much that I almost wanted it.

But it didn't. It stayed shockingly pliant, studying me with its furrowed brows. There was such a look in its eyes. Something I didn't want to name because I had a horrible feeling that the name might be *pity*.

It was unbearable, so I grabbed the body by the smooth globe of its shoulder and steered it up the stairs, pushing blindly through its foot-dragging stumbles, then up, again, hauling its corpse-stiff weight overhead. Shoved it, by the blue, bloodless soles of its feet, up the stepladder into my attic. I slammed the trapdoor shut and bolted it from the outside.

I made a last-ditch effort that week, a sort of frantic denial. Fighting the truth of what was happening.

I threw myself into the exhilarations of my new life, all the perks of this brand-new body. I ran until my lungs frayed, hiked until my feet were blistered and bleeding. I spent endless hours on the Tube, just for the sheer novelty of it, the unfathomable luxury of moving without thought. There was a certain thrill to commanding my own body, to no longer being dependent on the kindly whims of strangers. To not being stared at.

And then, at night, to be stared at altogether *differently*.

This, in particular, was a new dimension entirely. A plane of perception that I'd only been allowed a half-glimpse into before, now wide open and sprawling before me. It made me feel a little off-kilter to wander the world in my new body and find that it was an utterly different world from the one I had known.

I tried to convince myself that it was enough.

The first man I brought home was small, although still

a little taller than me, dense and wiry with round glasses that gave him a particularly intense look. He had a brown beard, thick enough to mask his expressions in a way that made me feel marginally less guilty about my own constructed inscrutability.

It felt so different now. More than anything else I had done, more than running or jumping or any other impossibilities, this – me against the wall with glasses-man's tongue in my mouth – was entirely alien, distinct from the experiences of before.

Before, this had been a plummeting leap, dropping from the sky with an unknowable parachute. It had become a survival exercise, a light-quick calculation of angles and landing ground, of desperate trust or the desperate lack of it.

There was none of that this time. Or almost none, with this shored-up body. No familiar edge of pain in the places his body pressed against mine.

I didn't know what to do with all the space in my brain now that I wasn't having to negotiate a shift towards the radiator so that I could perch and rest, or subtly ease his hands away from the feather-flesh of old surgical scars. Now that I wasn't pondering, in some dingy, primal part of my brain, how totally in command of his own muscles he was; how absolutely fucked I might be if this took any kind of turn, if I needed to run or fight or anything else that my body simply *couldn't*.

It was just blunt physicality now: the scratch of his

beard and the alien muscles of his lips, his tongue. Nice enough, of course. But something altogether different.

Often since the procedure, I had revelled in the novelty of this body's sensations. But on this night, for the first time since waking in the clinic, I was preoccupied with the gulf, the absence. Something was missing.

I felt it as a sudden grief. Or perhaps not so much grief as wrenching homesickness. I was twelve years old again, pleading to be brought home from a sleepover. I was four, banished back to my own cold bed in a monster-infested bedroom.

'Are you OK?'

Evidently, glasses-man had also noticed the floor plummeting out from under us, because he pulled back, looking worried.

I told him that I was fine, that I just needed a second. I walked into the kitchen and filled a glass with tepid water. I didn't drink it, just enjoyed the heaviness of it in my hands.

He followed me.

'I have to ask…' he started. He wore a look of put-on cheekiness that made me apprehensive. 'You're so perfect, and your skin and everything – I was wondering, have you, y'know…'

I played dumb.

'Have you had *it*?' His voice had lowered to a sharp, excitable whisper. 'I mean, no judgement here if you have – I've thought about it myself, y'know, get rid of the glass-es, maybe be a bit taller…'

I waited a long time in the vain hope that he would realise how uncomfortable I was and stop talking; or perhaps that he would miraculously lose his train of thought and forget the matter altogether.

When his eyes, magnified expectantly by his glasses, kept looking for their answer, I finally gave the smallest, least committal nod I could muster.

He let out a whistling breath.

'Oh my god,' he said. 'That is… I mean, what do your family think of that?'

I told him that my family weren't really in the picture. This did not deter him.

'Ah, right, sorry to hear that. But can I just ask…' He stepped closer to me.

Whatever he had wanted to ask would remain a mystery, because, just then, the house echoed with a great, concussive thump, forceful enough to rattle the plaster.

'What the fuck was that?'

The answer was another thump, and another. A series of thundering stamps, like the frantic floor-kick of a child's tantrum. So heavy that it made dust rain down on us, made the cobwebs collapse and crumble into a silver nothing.

I told him to wait and ran upstairs.

Whether out of some misguided chivalry or – as I suspected – curiosity, he ignored my instruction. I could hear him bounding up the steps behind me. His mouth was still spilling over with a breathless arrogance of questions.

As we got closer to the attic, the orchestra of chaos separated out. The thumps were punctuated with a feral scratching of fingernails against wood and, occasionally, a hideous opera, that wordless howl I had come to recognise in my very bones.

'Fucking hell,' the man said. 'Is that what I think it is?'

His voice had lost any fear; a smile was frothing at the upturned edges of his lips. A hungry smile, all ravenous curiosity, ready to consume me.

He rushed past me, heading straight for the stepladder. I heard myself, my carefully pathetic voice, stumbling through pleas and apologetic denials, but it was no use. He was already there, already throwing open the trapdoor and disappearing up into the attic.

I followed him, hit the light switch. It was a single bulb, dull and yellow. Barely-there light. But still, enough to see. Enough to do damage.

The body was kneeling on the floorboards before us. I could see the skin of its knuckles, torn and raw, the feeble scrapes of blood where it had been throwing its full weight at the floor, heedless to the blood, to the pain. Its hair was a riot of grease atop its head, and it was bruised, dishevelled – but it was still damningly recognisable. Still me.

'God,' the man said, shuffling closer. I could feel the heaviness of his boots on the floorboards. 'It really is you, isn't it? Mad.'

He stepped even closer, circling it now, prodding it every now and again with the toe of his boot.

'So what was wrong with you before? I mean, something's not right with it, right?'

He reached out then with careless fingers, poking at the top of the body's thigh.

'Stop it,' I said.

My voice surprised even me.

He looked back at me, a little coolly, eyebrows flicking up in mock surprise.

'Sorry,' he said, without any feeling at all. 'What, can you feel it, or something?'

Without waiting for me to reply, his fingers found the exposed flesh at the waist where the ragged T-shirt had fallen aside. He grabbed a pale roll of skin and pinched it, hard.

The body did not react. It hadn't even glanced at him, in fact. I felt a swell of unexpected pride.

It kept its eyes fixed on me, unblinking and solemn. I spoke again.

'I told you to stop it.'

He ignored me. I could see the body's jaw ticking, hands knotting up into fists. In that moment, we really were identical. In that moment, I didn't mind.

Now he was lifting her top, laughing stupidly as he did so. When I spoke again, my voice was different. Harder.

'Don't touch her.'

He finally stopped then. Raised his hands in performative surrender, donning a conciliatory expression as though to highlight just how hysterical and unreasonable I was being.

'Jesus, sorry,' he said, picking his way back over the floorboards towards me, coming to stand a little closer than I would have liked.

When he spoke again, his voice was all forced jocularity, tinged with a bitter half-laugh.

'For what it's worth, I can see why you wanted to get rid of it.'

The body acted quickly. Before I had fully understood the words, before they had even reached my ears, she had lunged, on her knees, teeth bared.

She was a fearsome thing, all determination and jutting bones, fury and awkward angles.

I knew, of course, the limits of that body, knew just how much weaker she would be than him – especially now, after weeks of damage. But her former docility had given her the element of surprise, and that was enough for her to put her plan into action.

He disappeared with an abruptness that was almost amusing. He didn't even have time to scream as he lurched backwards out of the open trapdoor, landing with a brutal thump.

It was silent in the attic. I realised that neither of us were breathing, both in the same terrible stasis as we waited to see if he would return, full of rage. If we would need to fight once more.

Below, I could hear him setting himself to rights – the

dragging of boots across the floorboards, the creaking of the ladder as he leant on it to stand. His panting breaths, ragged with rage.

Then an incoherent scream, billowing against the walls and around the house, followed swiftly by a volley of yelped obscenities.

Finally, the sound of his footsteps going back downstairs. The soft quake of the walls as the front door was swung wildly open and then slammed shut.

Breath tumbled from my lungs again. I didn't know what to do with myself. My body felt too loose. I stepped forward, carefully, to the edge of the trapdoor, easing myself to the floor. I sat with my legs dangling over the edge. I mapped their straightness, their obedience, their disconcerting grace where they rested in the empty air.

I was aware of the body shifting behind me, shuffling closer on her bloodied knees. I didn't turn around to look at her. I wanted to give her privacy, to let her do whatever she needed to. Wanted to offer her the smooth, unsuspecting plane of my back.

She settled herself beside me. She was sitting a little further back than I was, propped more securely away from the looming hollow in the floorboards. I understood. I remembered what it was to live in an unpredictable body.

She looked at me. I had never noticed the kindness of her eyes. She smiled her sweet, lopsided smile. The smile that had once been mine.

She reached out, put her hand on mine. It was warm.

It was slow, careful work, to put my body back together again. To run the bath, soak my hand in it, fumble for the lost skin-memory of how I had liked my baths before. What it was that my body wanted from the water. Remembering to add the near-luminous green bubble bath, our shared favourite.

It was difficult to get her back down from the attic, to guide her pointed feet from step to step. I had to hold her waist at times, take on some of her weight and ease it down to safety. Then the same process again, to lift her over the edge of the bathtub, ease her in softly, make sure I wasn't scalding her.

I worried that she would be frightened, that she would be tormented by the memories of drowning when the water touched her. But she relaxed right into it, head back like a baptism, the tips of her ears just kissing the water. She seemed to know I meant no harm. Perhaps it was because she knew me, had known me since before I was born, had always been with me. Or perhaps she was just the bravest part of me. Brave enough to trust.

The soap was a white bar, fresh from the pack. I started at her feet, lathering them with the stuff, working over the startlingly rigid muscles and tendons, prising open the clenched-up toes to wash away the dirt beneath. I washed her shins till the bruises shone, vivid, washed the soft fleshiness of her stomach and the sibilant curves of her spine. I lathered up her hair and rubbed it to the roots, rinsing it out with a plastic jug of water tipped so-gently, my hand above her eyes to shelter them.

When she is ready, I will wrap her in towels and carry her like a child. In my room, I will take an inventory of the damage I have done.

I will not apologise to her. Not because I am not sorry, but because words are no good between us.

Instead, I will trim her nails, free her fingertips from the grave-dirt and the blood. Softly, I will snip the burnt ends from her hair. I will wrap her broken bones tight in the softest bandages, hang her arm in a sling, anoint each bruise with arnica. For every scrape, a sticking plaster and a gentle kiss.

I do not know yet if this will be enough, if I will ever truly repair my library of self-inflicted wounds.

I hope I can.

The Merman

The window above Mrs Matthews's kitchen sink looks out over the cliffs, to the sea. If she leans forward, she can see all the way to the horizon. Her eyes are wide, as if to swallow the vastness of the sight, and her hands move unthinkingly through the lukewarm clattering of dishes. They have grown so weather-beaten over the decades that she no longer feels the heat of the water, the hidden sharpness of awkwardly lodged knives.

In the next room, the shipping forecast burbles out of the old wireless. *Humber, Thames, Dover. West or southwest four, becoming variable three or less, then east or southeast three or four later. In Dover, slight becoming smooth…*

She knows, without looking, that her husband will be sitting right beside it, so close that his good ear is almost pressed against the trembling mesh. Sometimes, he'll hold the stub of a pencil in his hand, making notes in indecipherable handwriting. His memory isn't so good these days, and he likes to pore over them later on, in the lengthy, quiet stretches between broadcasts.

It's her favourite kind of day today, the sort of weather not everyone would recognise as beautiful. The sky is as pale as a cataract and there is a flinty solidity to the softly shifting edges of the waves. Only a true observer of the sea, an old friend, could note the velvety blue hidden in the depths, appearing as a sudden flash now and then, like a jay's prized feather. The unthinkable vastness of it, the astonishing, violent beauty, pulls the air out of her lungs. She can never quite bring herself to hate the sea, even now.

She starts to prepare the breakfast things, anxiously smoothing out the creases of a fresh gingham cloth, setting out half a loaf of crusty bread and a china dish of soft, yellow butter. By now, she can hear the tentative padding of Mr Matthews's brogues over the linoleum as he comes to sit down beside her. Like her, he always dresses well: braces, a carefully ironed shirt the delicate blue of a duck's egg. She notices his tie, a navy, woollen thing she knitted for him fifty years ago. Adorning it, the anchor tiepin, painstakingly polished but slightly askew. Beloved gift of a long-ago Father's Day.

On autopilot, she straightens it (her hands are better than his, if only barely) and smooths down a stubborn, bed-swept tuft of his white hair, as though he is just another part of the tablecloth. He looks up at her and smiles, a careworn thing of absolute familiarity. They settle themselves on their creaking chairs – two occupied, one empty.

Bread and butter, and good, strong tea without sugar. Her hands tremble a little as she lifts the burnished teapot to pour, partaking in that age-old, carry-on ritual.

Without the radio or the clattering of wet china, a keen, almost *expectant* silence settles over the room. Their hopeful neatness, the oh-so-careful way in which they lift their teacups to their lips, makes it seem as though they are listening out for something, anticipating the footsteps of some much-awaited visitor towards their front door.

But, of course, nobody ever comes. There is only silence.

After breakfast, they take their usual walk. Her husband proffers his arm, as if squiring her to a dance, to support her a little as they set out along the clifftop path. (His legs are better than hers, if only barely.)

Their eyes never stray on these walks. Not for a moment. They never glance up at the gulls wheeling in the blank sky overhead, or the sandy path in front them, or at the strong, shiny clifftop grass that flickers in the wind like loose cassette tape.

No – they are laser focused, like the very best lookouts, their eyes shining with a new clarity as they pierce the overwhelming swathes of ocean and shore. There is a defiant set to their arthritic shoulders as they brace against the wind.

Such is their daily routine, their pilgrimage, a journey that has been carved, over lonely decades, into their very bones. Tens of thousands of empty searches, and still, each morning, they set out and scour the sea like distant beachcombers.

And then, today – *something*.

She spots it first: a form, a body, entangled and flung into such disarray that it is hardly recognisable as such. But she is sure that she sees something, a sort of ragged, flesh-coloured bundle, huddled on the stones at the edge of the shore. And around its head (or what she imagines to be a head), a splash of black hair, spilled ink-dark on the pale rock.

She runs, breaking away from her husband, heedless of her precarious balance and the ruthless sharpness of the rocks and the plummeting steepness of the cliffs, scrambling, clawing tufts of grass with her as she half falls.

Each lurching step seems to slough a year off her; by the time she reaches the shore, she is as sprightly as a newly-wed.

Mr Matthews, who has spotted nothing at all, nonetheless follows his wife as quickly as his knees will permit.

As she nears the body, she realises, with a great tugging at the base of her ribcage, that her observations were both right and wrong, that what lies before her is both a body and, impossibly, *not*.

At a distance, the sight is easy enough to grasp. A tall man, naked, with a head of dark curls and an untamed beard which lends a wildness to him. He is caught, broken-limbed and bleeding, in a cruelly barbed span of fishing net.

But as she gets nearer, as her ever-scouring eyes take in the hyper-reality of him, the jarring, impossible details, the overall effect is… She grapples for the word.

Uncanny, she realises, as she trails her gaze over his slightly-too-large body. As she notes the silvery sheen of water rolling effortlessly off the hair on his chest and stomach; the little limpets and barnacles that are encrusted, like oceanic acne, into his shoulders, his cheeks, the hollows of his collarbones. He is uncanny.

And his eyes – strangest of all things – his eyes are *shipwreck coloured.*

Five seconds. She allows herself five seconds to feel the great tidal surge of fear rush over her, to acknowledge, and swiftly disregard, the urge to run.

Because he is still breathing – great, rattling, sick-bay breaths, those of a half-drowned man – and so she has a job to do.

She was a nurse a long time ago, in the navy, and so her body remembers how to kneel in a pool of blood, how to breathe in the scent of diseased flesh without gagging. She knows exactly the right weight to put behind a comforting hand, and all the best soothing nonsense to whisper in the ear of a nameless boy, far from home.

She pries out the rusted fishhook which has lodged itself in his left gill, that soft, open gland in the side of his neck, flaring gently with his every faltering breath. Then she mops up the pus and blood with the hankie from her sleeve, and she does not flinch.

(It's true the boys she cared for back then didn't have gills, but she has seen the lost look in his eyes and the shoddiness of his beard and has decided, pragmatically, that a boy is a boy, regardless of species.)

Mr Matthews stands a distance behind her now, watching dumbly, fumbling with the sheer strangeness of the sight before him. But he, too, is seized by a very old, very profound instinct, and he rushes to his wife's side, stumbling into a crouch by the merman's head.

It is the very gentlest of muscle memories that brings his arthritic hand to that dark, sea-soaked hair, which moves it through the hesitant, paternal strokes. There is a lullaby on his lips, although his voice is too quiet to be heard over the roar of the wind and sea.

By now she is working the creature free of the net, tearing apart the toughened nylon with nails, teeth, a sharp stone, clawing him out with an almost frantic determination. In places, the cords have dug right into the flesh of his limbs, leaving them bloody, his feet grey from lack of circulation. Laying on his side now, he curls deeper into himself. His lips – worryingly, she notes they're slightly blue, and swollen like a corpse's – are pursed up, as though he's crying, but no tears fall from his strange eyes.

Finally, he is free, and it's only then that she notices that her hands are skinned and keen and delicate like raw meat; only then that she begins to feel the ache of cold and exhaustion seep into her entire being. But she can't indulge it, not yet; she can't give in – the greater part of the rescue is still ahead of them. They must somehow get him up the cliff to safety.

Slowly, unsteadily, she eases herself up, brushing her skirt down with her hands. Her husband is doing the same, pushing himself up, his hands against his knees, trying not to topple over onto the unforgiving stone.

Then they each reach a hand down to the merman and, in the universal language of their kind eyes, entreat him to stand, to walk.

Everything depends on this. He's still too injured, it seems, to swim safely out to sea; he must convalesce on land. But there's no question of their carrying him – he's bigger than the both of them put together, and even as a shared effort it would be an impossibility. There's no telephone nearby and, even if there was, there's a sort of unspoken acknowledgement between the two of them that to alert anybody else to this creature's plight would be a dangerous prospect.

The merman must stand or die.

He stands. Slowly, unnaturally, like a child taking their very first steps. It's abundantly clear that the action is alien to him, or at least very long neglected. He throws one vast arm over each of his rescuers, and together they climb.

Each step is a war, tactically assessed, battling against pain and stiff sinew, full of unforeseen risk. But the three of them are all mining that untapped inner strength, the immense and secret reserves of those who have no choice.

By the time they reach the house, the sun has passed its peak and is making its own homeward journey. The merman almost collapses through the front door as it gives way, and his weight is nearly unbearable as they half drag him through the kitchen and usher him, scrabbling on his hands and feet, up the narrow, carpeted staircase.

There are two bedrooms in their house. They bring him into the second.

As he finally collapses into unconsciousness, they ease him into the bed that has been waiting, painstakingly made, for forty years.

For three days or so, he wavers, an uncertain guest on the doorstep of their lives. For three days, those strange, beautiful eyes of his are unfocused, and there are lengthy, tense hiatuses in his breathing. For three days, a tender improvisation of care, as they learn all the quirks of this brand-new, ancient body.

Fresh water scalds him, but a soft flannel soaked in seawater seems to soothe his pains. He gags on tea and broth but draws, desperately, on hot brine, delivered to his lips through the spout of their second-best teapot.

The morning after his arrival, Mrs Matthews sets to work in earnest: sponging off the most gaping and filthy of his wounds, detangling barbed hooks and jagged plastic. Stitching the merman back together as deftly as her shaking hands will allow.

Her fingertips become familiar with the protruding barnacles that pucker his flesh, with the oddly waxy, impenetrable quality of his skin, with his stubble, which is as shockingly rough as a cat's tongue. She expects to be repulsed at first, feeling his differences so fully and so intimately, but it isn't like that – not at all. All she feels is the profound, thrilling curiosity of absolute novelty, and a hint of something more: a rich upwelling of familiar comfort that she cannot quite name. A kind of recognition.

All day, her husband races up and down the narrow staircase with endless offerings of saline, gauze, sticking plaster. When it is clear there is nothing more he can contribute, he paces outside the bedroom door, like a father outside the delivery room.

Late that night, as the merman flickers in and out of being, they kneel beside his bed – this couple with creaking knees, who recognise no god – and send a frantic prayer to nobody in particular. *Save him. Save him.*

The ocean itself delivers benediction, because, on the morning of the spring tide, he takes a turn for the better. His eyes are clearer than they have ever been; there is a hint of dawn-pink to his lips. His skin is still barnacled, still seawater-mottled to the touch, but it is also warm. And the old couple can sleep, at last, because the rhythm of his breaths from the next room is strong and unwavering.

On the third day of his recovery, he wanders into the kitchen, silently stooping through the doorway and standing there uncertainly. She doesn't see him to begin with, focused as she is on the dishwater-coloured horizon, on the teacups, warm and humming on the draining board.

He comes a little further into the room. Every sinew of him is apologetic somehow, as though he is aware of his own vastness and attempting desperately to make himself smaller, less imposing. With some relief, she sees that he is no longer naked. He is wearing the clothes they left folded on a chair in his bedroom: a thick gansey jumper and striped pyjama bottoms which flap stupidly around his mid-calves.

He looks a little embarrassed by her prolonged staring, so she turns away, back to the task at hand – drying the cups, putting them away. She makes a great performance of casualness, but all the while is keenly conscious of him behind her, his breath strong, his salt-wild hair almost brushing the Artex ceiling.

He moves about strangely, she thinks. He walks slightly on his heels, with an imitative stiffness, like some black-and-white rendition of Frankenstein's monster. There's a childlike unsteadiness which belies his height, his beard and sinew, the maturity of his body. He doesn't walk like a man with a lifetime of experience in the act.

She's craning upwards, teetering as she reaches to a high shelf, when, without being asked, he steps forward and takes the cup from her, slotting it easily into place. He waits there, with open hands and expectant eyes, until she hands him the next teacup, which he likewise puts away. There's soon a nice rhythm between them, in this companionable passing of cups. He is so very careful, handling each item as if it were the most precious of treasures.

When the work is done, he closes the cabinet door and leans down to drop a quiet kiss onto the top of her head, smiling into her silver hair. She finds herself wondering then – how did such a wild creature learn to love so perfectly?

For dinner that night, her husband dons his rain mac against the endless drizzle and fights his way down the cliff path to the town. He returns not quite an hour later with fish and chips, steaming hot and wrapped in newspaper. He has bought more than their usual portion – far more, enough to raise a few eyebrows – even though, he realises with some apprehension, he has no idea what, or even if, the merman likes to eat.

At first, he chews on it open-mouthed, jaw slack in horror at the alien heat that scalds his gums, the dry, sharp edges of batter, the unmistakeably human flavour of grease. There is something profoundly toddlerish about the way he furrows his brow, knots up his still-blue lips in displeasure. Captured on his bearded face, the expression is a juxtaposition so gloriously silly that Mrs Matthews lets out a sudden shriek of laughter. It really is a shriek too, a wild, uninhibited sound, the sort of noise she might have made as a teenager.

He jumps at that, eyes pale and wide, afraid he's caused offence, but when he sees the grin spreading across the room – seeping from her face onto Mr Matthews's – he joins in. A strange, silent laugh, but unrestrained, his great shoulders shaking, his eyes crinkled at the corners, his lips smiling wide to expose sharp, pearlescent teeth. They are all so consumed by their laughter that soon the cutlery is clattering on the Ercol table between them, great drops of water splashing out of the water jug and onto the tablecloth.

As the last giggles subside, the merman makes another valiant attempt at his food. In a moment of brilliance, Mr Matthews nudges the salt cellar towards him.

Gently, so gently, the merman takes it from him, the coral stubs of his fingernails scratching against the old metal as he curls his too-large hands awkwardly around it. He tips out a few grains of salt onto his fingertip, lifts the finger to his lips and presses it against his outstretched tongue. The sea-foam whites of his eyes shoot wide in a kind of delighted recognition. Without stopping to ask for permission, without so much as even a faltering glance their way, he unhinges his vast mouth and tips the salt directly into it. They watch the white grains pour out in a continuous stream, pooling into a little heap on his tongue.

He swallows hard, a great rolling swell of his Adam's apple, and then beams at them. He is, Mrs Matthews thinks, visibly revived. His skin is less wan, freshly gleaming with saltwater dew. The oceanic debris which clings to him, the little shells and barnacles and chips of coral, are far more vibrant than they were before. Healthy.

For once, he doesn't seem to notice their amazed stares, wholly immersed as he is in his own delight. He is studying his meal again, prodding past the chips and the grease-soaked paper to prise apart the fish with a scientific air. He leans forward, giving it a careful sniff.

Then, resolved, he begins his operation, carefully peeling back the batter, excavating tiny chunks of pure white cod. He pulls them apart very carefully, until they are barely intact, so soft as to look half chewed. To complete the process, he smothers it all in salt, so that every single strand of fish is thickly crystalline with the stuff, almost more powder than food.

He eats. First falteringly, then with a ravenous glee. There's something distinctly animalistic about the way he claws the fish between his fingers and crams it into his mouth, the occasional habit he has of spitting forcefully onto his plate and muddling the white foam up together with his food. The effect of all of this is only heightened by the fact that he seems, somehow, to be smiling *while* he's eating, so that all his teeth are bared into an unintentional snarl.

Looking on, Mr and Mrs Matthews feel, for the very first time, a twinge of disgust. Here, at his most unguarded, he is fully exposed as *creature*, not man. His vulnerability is repulsive. They feel it as a physical presence, like the fleshy underside of some armoured creature, like a squelching invertebrate prised from its shell. The merman has thrown off the last of his protective casing, exposed the uttermost extremities of his strangeness, and there is a sudden, reflexive impulse to squash him. It would be so easy.

But then he smiles at them – sweet, guileless, breathless with joy – and the feeling is gone.

It never returns.

They know how to feed him properly after that. They start buying up more salt than the shops can stock, enough to prompt remarks, several uninventive quips about the old man's heart and blood pressure. Behind closed doors, the conversations are both more earnest and more dangerous – little conferences about the couple's sudden secrecy, their fits of 'eccentric behaviour'.

All thickly laced with false concern, of course.

The Matthewses cannot bring themselves to mind, though, so enthralled are they by the merman's stunning recuperation. If they had imagined him to be getting stronger before, it is nothing to this – his sudden buoyancy, his irrepressible energy. His old timidity is all but gone; he no longer shrinks into himself, no longer treads so quietly along the carpeted halls. He smiles more, even when he doesn't know they are looking.

He is much more like his old self, Mr Matthews catches himself thinking one day, before he realises that neither of them can claim to know what his 'old self' had been, can even begin to imagine the aquatic life he might have led before he washed up in their lives. Yet the statement rings true, all the same.

There is something so beautiful about it.

One night, a fortnight after they first spotted him splayed across the shore, they gather together in the front room. The lamps lend a plush, orange cast to the evening, and the old couple gorge themselves happily on a box of sticky, liquor-filled chocolates wrapped in gold paper. On a whim, Mr Matthews drags out the old gramophone, thumbing through dusty vinyls while the merman, puzzled, crouches on the floor opposite him and runs his fingers over the indents in the carpet where it has borne the gramophone's weight for so long.

Mr Matthews, having chosen a record, carefully blows the dust from it and eases it onto the machine, his tongue poking out from between his teeth as he sets it straight. He picks up the needle but fumbles it, so that it drops hard onto the edge of the record and makes the merman jump. For a moment there is quiet – just the soft hearth-crackling of the LP and the potential space of music-to-be.

Then it starts up – a creaking swell of violins; the compacted memory of a long-dead orchestra. There is a short, swooping instrumental opening, and then a man begins to sing. His voice is deep and somehow old-fashioned.

La mer
Qu'on voit danser
Le long des golfes clairs

The old couple begin to dance, swaying almost in time to the music. They are out of practice: their bodies bump into each other, and Mrs Matthews giggles as her husband steps on her toes. At one point, he raises their joined hands, and it takes a faltering moment for her to react, to remember what to do – ducking beneath his arm in a doddering twirl, crashing into his jumper-clad chest and planting a firm kiss on his cheek while she's there.

So absorbed are they in this act of rediscovery that they lose sight of their merman; by the time they notice him, the song is on its final refrain.

The merman is always silent, of course, but now he seems to *absorb* sound, to swallow it up like a great blank void, like the very depths of the ocean. He is unfeasibly still, half crouching, half sitting, barefoot on the carpet, exactly where they left him; he does not even seem to be breathing. Mrs Matthews looks closely and sees that there is no tell-tale flaring of his gills as the air rattles through them.

Only his fingers, outstretched, offer any sign of life. They are trembling ever so slightly, as though he is trying to trace the strands of the music in the air; as though he wants to grasp it in his hands.

His eyes are wide and oddly heavy. She thinks that if he could cry tears, he would be doing so now.

The old song dies and another starts up. A waltz.

The merman is still frozen in awe. Slowly, carefully, Mrs Matthews approaches him and offers her hand.

For a time, he looks up at her, uncomprehending, but then he engulfs her hand with his own. The weight of it, the density, is shocking – as though he is solid all the way through, his very bones nothing but rock.

The merman unfolds himself until he is standing before her. Waiting there, his arms suspended at uncertain angles, his eyes vast, he looks precisely like every boy she has ever danced with. If his panic didn't seem so earnest, she could almost laugh at him.

She doesn't laugh. Instead, they dance. Or they attempt a dance. Between her arthritic joints and his first-day-on-Earth posturing, their quiet back-and-forth shuffle doesn't hold any recognisable grace.

But their arms are entangled, and they are smiling softly at one another and together allowing the ebb and flow of the music to carry them where it may.

It isn't until he presses a little closer to her, bowing his back so that he shelters her almost entirely, that she hears the sound.

It's a sort of humming, but to call it humming would be a disservice. It's deeper than deep, with a church-choir resonance that cuts to the core of her. It's so powerful that she is sure she can feel her very atoms vibrate and yet, simultaneously, it is as soft as the whispers you hear in shells.

The merman's voice is a beautiful thing.

His mouth, she notices, is positioned towards her left side – her dullest ear, stopped up with a hearing aid. Yet there are no protesting squeals of feedback as his lips brush ever closer, and his song holds none of the artificial quality she is used to.

Very quickly, she ascertains that this is no human sound. This is something more than vocal muscles and moving air; this is the language of another universe entirely. Breathless, wordless. Truer than speech.

A glance at her husband confirms the theory – even all the way across the room, where his own long-muffled ears could never possibly catch any ordinary noise, he is stock-still, staring at the merman with tears in his eyes. He, too, hears the song, even if his ears are none the wiser.

When they finally retire, the merman continues his strange song long into the night. Comfortable in their half-sleep, they let it carry them away.

They are old, and so they are full of old songs.

Mrs Matthews gives the merman Sunday School hymns, a handful of lullabies, perhaps the odd love song from her youth. Mr Matthews is particularly fond of sea shanties, and bawdy ballads with lyrics he's glad the merman can't repeat. They both love folk songs, with half-forgotten words they have to cobble together, carving scraps of rhyme and refrain from the broadest strokes of a story.

The merman's own voice seems to get stronger with every note they send his way, gorging itself on their unsteady melodies and growing into a force that shakes the house to its foundations.

They spend days on end this way, throwing everything they can into the great echo-cave of his body, delighting in the unexpected returns.

At first, he provides only an imitation – an echo of sorts, although it is so much richer than their own creaking voices that they're half convinced his music must somehow pre-exist their own. That they, and not him, are the echoes.

Soon enough his voice presses further, into fragments of song that they have never heard before – which, they suspect, nobody has ever heard before. Some of the notes are recognisable but some are entirely alien, entities that could never be captured on any human stave. Inarticulable.

None of his songs have words, of course, but they have meanings of a kind. Mr Matthews fancies that he can see them sometimes, in sudden flashes of brilliance. Great swelling storms caving over old square-riggers. Treasure sinking into ink-dark depths.

One afternoon, almost a month after the rescue, finds them sitting listening to him in the kitchen. The place is all golden light and forgotten tea left to steep too long. Even the dust in the air seems to sway to the currents of his voice.

Then, a knock.

It is soft at first. A mere scuffle against the thick double-glazing of the door panels. It could be anything; for a glorious second, it seems that they can ignore it, and that the merman's song can continue uninterrupted, and everything will stay just as it has been.

Another knock. This one far harder, far more insistent. Mrs Matthews flinches at the crack of bone against glass before she bustles over to answer.

Their voices are just a murmuring to begin with, but then they crescendo. There are panicked edges in Mrs Matthews's speech, sharp tones she has never used with her husband, or with her merman.

Then footsteps, loud and getting ever louder. An army of booted feet, tracking in dirt across the spotless carpets, toppling dishes and ornaments in their wake.

There are five of them, three men and two women, all crowded in and seemingly unconcerned with the obscene amount of space they take up. They wear uniform expressions of all-consuming, uncomprehending disgust as they set eyes on the scene in front of them.

Mr Matthews thinks, with a vast and boundless bitterness, that they ought to have come brandishing pitchforks.

The merman, his eyes open wounds, turns to look at them. He is clutching the back of his chair like a child. When Mrs Matthews remembers this terrible day later, she will be haunted by the whiteness of his knuckles.

The man at the front of the pack steps forward, lifting slightly onto his tiptoes in an effort to make himself seem taller. He is about sixty years old, with a plump face and pale, diffuse eyebrows. He does not look cruel. Mrs

Matthews realises, too weary now to even be surprised, that he is her GP.

And then he opens his mouth. His voice is the ugliest sound they have ever heard.

'What the hell,' he asks, 'is that *thing*?'

All of this has happened before.

The merman is familiar with cruel human hands, with what it means to be ripped from his home. His body remembers the beatings and the broken glass; it still bears the scars of centuries-old binds and the wrath of generations long since dead.

Even the oldest humans are young to him, so when the vicar, pale with age, suggests that they lock the creature in the crypt of his church, he does not know that history is repeating itself. Does not know that he is just another turn in the endless cycle of human disappointment.

The merman is stronger than any of them and yet he just follows meekly, like a little mooncalf destined for drowning.

The crypt is cold, with air so stagnant that it feels stone-thick against his skin. He can smell the bone dust muddled into the cement of the place, the lingering tang of the blood-iron.

He can feel the misery of the church, the intolerance of the very stone itself where it lies cold against the unbending earth. He is astonished by how little has changed since the last time he was here. He feels a spasm of homesickness then, for the protean ocean, for its infinite malleability.

They bring him a jug of water, but it is freshwater, and so it burns his throat, brings his lips out in blisters. The merman pretends not to see the little sparks of hungry fascination in the blue eyes of the doctor when this happens. Even he can only tolerate so much dread in one day.

Later, there is food: some sort of brown stew, oil-slick with a thick, savoury smell. The merman knows that he should eat, can feel his strength ebbing. But the merest touch of it upon his lips proves it to be earthy and bloody and saltless, and his body rebels, retching.

The woman who brought the food – a teacher, he's gathered, cardigan-clad, wearing a large, raggedy felt brooch – watches him. Her smile curdles and she shakes her head in disbelief. He is mesmerised by the little silver cross she wears on a chain around her neck, by the way it dances about as she moves. He wonders what it means.

In the second he is distracted, she's on her feet and moving towards him, her arm outstretched. He looks up at her, unmoving, not sure what to expect. Like a too-tame animal who has not known hunters. Almost, if not quite, trusting; his survival instincts eroded by centuries of peace.

First, she seizes the food from his unresisting grip, hurling it at the crypt wall behind his head. The cheap plastic of the bowl clatters against ancient bones, food seeping down the walls. The explosion of the stew's scent – newly disrupted – is repulsive to him, but the sight is oddly mesmeric.

Then the woman brings her hand back down across his face. Hard. Very hard. Hard enough to force his jaw back towards her, so that he is facing her once again; hard enough to draw blood where her fussy, gem-encrusted rings have cut through his skin.

He has known violence before, of course, so the prickling white heat, the apparent looseness of his eye in its socket, is no surprise to him. Yet he had almost forgotten the suddenness of pain. How instantaneously it snaps itself into existence. How relentlessly it demands his attention.

Her eyes are cold and oddly shuttered, but there's something about the curve of her lips that speaks to a joy, or at least a self-satisfaction, at having administered punishment.

She turns to leave. Her gait is light, jaunty. The cross swings about on her neck as she goes.

Early the next morning, the doctor returns. His hair is still sleep rumpled at the back and there is a speck of shaving foam on his jaw. When he kneels down beside the merman, he sets aside his medical bag and a travel mug full of coffee, still too hot to drink.

Then, with slow exactness, he lays out his tools. Scalpels and syringes and rubber tourniquets. Cotton wool and gauze and plastic sample bags. A tinkling of glass tubes and specimen beakers.

For a naïve, fleeting moment, the merman thinks that perhaps the doctor is about to tend to his wounds, as Mrs Matthews had done. But the odds of this hope do not tally well with what he already knows about this doctor, about *humans*. Nor with the sharpness of these tools, and the grim look on the man's face.

He begins with the tourniquet. Too tight around the merman's right arm, pinching pale flesh and squeezing sea-blue veins to a bulge.

The needle is a new sensation to the merman, the dry, searing sting of it. He watches his blood – not red human blood, but wine-dark – sputter out of the valve and into a plastic tube. Then another, and another again, more of his own blood than he has ever seen. He thinks, *He is never going to stop*; thinks, *This will surely sink me.*

And still, he does not fight. Still, he closes up his lonely eyes under pale lids and leans himself back against the wall of bones. He feels the rushing in his ears and tries to imagine white horses crashing into the crypt, flooding it, drowning out everything else.

There's a very noble look to him in that half-there haze. He looks like a knight in an epic painting, every inch the wounded soldier. Primed for his sainthood.

The doctor doesn't notice, of course, because now he has turned to his scalpels, and his fingertips are quivering with barely suppressed glee.

He brings his hands to the merman's arm, but this time he traces all the way up to his shoulders (the borrowed jumper long since torn aside). His fingers dance over the barnacles and limpets and encrusted weeds, the places where the skin is scarred and puckered like coral.

He raises the scalpel. It scratches lightly against the hard, organic surface.

Then he lodges it beneath one of the largest barnacles. Pushing with his other hand, he begins, painstakingly, to *prise*.

The merman didn't know his body could feel like this. Like a soft, open eye socket ground with broken glass. Like an exposed nerve cut right through the middle. Like every tooth in his skull rotting hollow all at once.

He screams. There is no sound, but the pressure of the room changes. He can see the doctor's throat working as he swallows, the unconscious cocking of his head as if trying to dislodge water from his ears. The little church crypt seems to sink ever further underground. The air hangs heavy on the doctor's bones.

The merman's own body contorts, curling in on itself, his spine pressing so desperately outwards that it seems it will break the skin. The muscles of his neck are broiling and writhing as he shouts his nothingness into existence.

The doctor shakes himself and pushes on. The merman watches as he finally wrenches the barnacle free and raises it to eye level, studying it with a small smile. Then he pops it into a specimen jar. The merman hears the clattering sound as it lands, can see where the pale tendrils of residual flesh are pressing damply against the side of the glass.

He takes more. A fingernail, wrenched right from the bed, leaving his fingertip open and weeping. A lock of hair snipped from his head. At one point, he lifts a plastic tube to the merman's lips and entreats him to spit, which he does, perhaps a little more forcefully than is strictly necessary.

He labels everything with a chewed-up ballpoint pen. Patient name, nature of sample, time of extraction. His tongue is poking out between his teeth as he focuses.

In all his interminable life, the merman has never felt more like a *thing* than he does in this moment.

With the pain comes knowledge, just as inescapable. He can feel it carving itself indelibly onto every bone in his body. He will never leave this place. Even if he is freed, even if he makes it back to the ocean, some part of him will always be here, buried alive and bleeding.

No matter how far he runs, this is where he will return to. This is what will be waiting for him in the night, when he is alone.

The doctor is packing up his tools now, shuffling needles into a sharps bin, wrapping bloodied cloths in plastic before he discards them. He straightens out his shirt, takes a slug of his coffee. The merman can see his face slacken as the thrill of this morning leaves him, as he prepares for another airless day in his surgery.

Before he goes, he turns to the merman a final time and catches sight of something. His gaze is critical, professional. Quickly, habitually, he opens his bag again and brings out a first-aid kit.

He lifts practised hands to the merman's face, to the place where the teacher's ring had cut him. It is still split, weeping.

The doctor cleans it first with an antiseptic wipe. The merman flinches at the sting but can feel that this is an altogether different vintage of pain, something distinct from the juddering, directionless nausea of before.

Then he begins to fix the cut, applying sticky strips of a dressing in place of stitches. It's delicate work; his tongue makes a reappearance as he fumbles through it.

The doctor's breath is very warm and smells of coffee. The merman is stunned by the softness of his fingertips, by how very fleshy and blunt they feel. He is close enough to see the liquid hues of the man's eyes, to notice that his eyelashes are short and much fairer than the rest of his hair. He looks away, downward, and sees a few creases across his shirt, unnoticed in the morning rush.

When the doctor pulls away, the merman ghosts his own fingertips (so much rougher) over his cheek. The skin there feels tight and safe. He can feel the orderly lines of the strips, can feel how carefully each one has been placed.

The doctor stands up. He gives the merman a brief, comforting smile. It is as if he has forgotten, momentarily, exactly what his patient is.

This, the merman thinks, is perhaps the greatest cruelty of humans. They won't even let you hate them properly.

The merman sleeps after that, but not well. He is always half aware of his body. It's a confusion of sensations, his cheek warm and healing even as his other wounds fester.

He had hoped that he would become faint soon from pain and hunger and blood loss, that he could let himself be carried off by the strange, floating sensation of half-consciousness, but the opposite is true. The merman feels even more firmly anchored to the earth, is hyper-aware of every point at which his body leans into the unforgiving ground.

The world around him remains stubbornly real.

The crypt is pitch-black, a darkness so entire that it seems to press close against him, nudging his closed lips and invading his nostrils. Time has long since disintegrated there in the dark, so he has no idea how long it has been – hours, days, centuries – when he hears the sound.

This place had seemed impenetrable, a great enclosed nothingness. When it first starts up, he is sure it is only his loneliness singing out to him. Only his own addled mind, which so often conjures up unfamiliar songs.

But when he lies his head still and focuses absolutely on the oh-so-distant strain of the music, he realises the truth. He can make out the oddly feeble vibrations of voice through cold church air, so different from his own people's song. Within the cluster of voices, he can hear all the little individual fallibilities. A few sore throats. Here and there, a childish treble lisping over unfamiliar words.

At least one person who seems not to have any grasp of the tune at all.

In the most wishful recesses of his imagination, he even thinks he hears *familiar* voices. The voices he loves the most, longs for. Thin with age and worry now.

Abide with me; fast falls the eventide…

It sounds strange to him, all those discordant voices in unison, all those weaknesses left on display – but it's a beautiful strangeness. So, too, is the crude physicality of it, palpable vibrations of air and stone.

Where he's lying on the floor, he shifts one hand free of his body and presses his palm against the ground, hard. He feels his knuckles stretch and splay, feels the barely-there warmth being drawn out of his exposed skin.

And then he feels, or imagines he feels, the humming of the stonework, rich with centuries of song. Lets himself enjoy it, all of those voices, joining the distant chorus above, swelling into a great choir of the living and the long since dead.

Against all sense, the merman *smiles*. His eyes flutter closed. He lets his bones sink into stillness.

Then the door bursts open with a surge of white light which eviscerates everything, blazing it into non-existence. Instinctively, he grinds the heels of his hands into his eye sockets, protecting them.

When, at last, he opens his eyes again, he is met with the smiling faces of Mr and Mrs Matthews.

Her knees have not improved at all since that day she first found him – if anything, these cold weeks have worsened them, the joints swelling and stiffening.

You wouldn't know it, though, watching her race across the crypt, collapsing to a kneel beside her merman. Reckless, unhesitating. Heedless of the pain.

His clothes are so torn that he is mostly naked, and he smells of sickness and dust. Many of his open wounds are ringed now in a vivid, venomous white. Lips the colour of the stone. Stretched out as he is, he is almost the full length of the room – his hair brushes the wall at one end, and his toes can just about reach the opposite end of his cell. He is terrifyingly pale.

Mrs Matthews wants to cry when she sees him, and perhaps would, if they only had the time. He looks even sicker, even wilder and more wounded than he did on that very first day, and she wonders, with a great swell of guilt, whether they should have left him well alone.

Then, when he looks at them both and just blinks and blinks as if he does not recognise them, she wonders, far more urgently, whether they are too late.

But then he smiles – a beautiful white flash of a smile, like a wave breaking – and they can all breathe again, if only briefly.

Because they have a job to do.

Mrs Matthews would love to revel in the joy of this

reunion, as her husband is, weeping and pressing his face into the merman's wayward curls. But her touches, though loving, are all purposeful. She maps his body, taking stock of the injuries, the places where infection has already begun to take hold. With a certain shrewdness in her eyes, she is already calculating his heft, the force it will take to get him standing on his feet. How they'll keep him upright once he gets there.

She draws in a great, shaking breath before they begin, steeling herself. There is no time for fear.

Her husband hears her and knows innately what must be done, getting on to his own feet, brushing off his knees and then freeing his hands. He stands there with them open, ready to catch or help or fight, ready to do whatever is needed.

Mrs Matthews, looking, thinks that perhaps this is what love is. Those upturned palms, patient, waiting.

The merman is pulling himself up now, using both of them and the walls. At one point he nearly falls, only saving himself by latching his hand around the yellowed globe of a skull, and they all send a private thought of thanks to the dead.

The merman looks again at that skull once he is upright. He wonders if he ever crossed paths with the owners of these bones the last time he was here; or whether those bodies are even more deeply buried, even further beyond reach.

As he casts a last glance around that crypt, he feels the full loneliness of eternity, just for a moment. Then Mr Matthews takes his hand.

Their plan has a loose shape. To retrieve him from the crypt during the Sunday morning service and sneak him out before the hymns are over, into the back car park. To settle him in their little car, which waits, diligently filled up with fuel, three carefully packed suitcases sitting quietly in the boot. And a shoebox beside them, containing just a few irreplaceables – photos, toys. All the rest they will leave behind for good.

From there they will drive – even they are not sure where. Away from this village, with all its hidden cruelty. To somewhere new, somewhere unhaunted.

But they do not make it that far. They are only halfway to the car when a voice cuts through the silence.

'Stop! I said stop!'

It is the vicar who shouts, but there are countless others who now spill out across the gravel to chase them down, or else to spectate. The whole congregation. Amongst them, familiar faces – the doctor, arms outstretched as if to corral a wild animal. The teacher, chin raised, shielding her children theatrically behind her. Postmen. Shopkeepers.

Mr and Mrs Matthews stop. They look over the crowd, at their blank, indistinguishable prejudice. They have known these people for decades. All of them are strangers.

The merman keeps running, reaching the car, slamming into it in his haste. The sleek metal shell is alien to him and he claws at it desperately, trying to reach anything he might dig his hands into, any place to hide. He finds the door handle and yanks at it with such frantic force that the car rocks on its tyres. The alarm shrieks out in a tantrum of orange lights.

The onlookers begin to laugh. The sound is cold and discordant. Mr Matthews sees their snarling teeth and thinks that he might be sick.

The merman slumps over the car, his brow pressed down against the roof. His back is still turned to the crowd.

He doesn't see who throws the first stone. It's a weak throw and hits him low, near his hipbone. Perhaps it was one of the children.

It bounces off harmlessly, this scrap of gravel, but it does start a trend. Others follow suit. Some work with sharp precision, aiming carefully at his eyes, his mouth, his wounds, all the soft, open places. Some throw the gravel in great, reckless handfuls.

At first it is sport, and they are still laughing and laughing as the stones rain down in a confetti of bruises. The Matthewses' pleas are lost in the cacophony.

But the merman is immoveable, the stones skimming right off him. He turns to face the onslaught and stands solid, shoulders as broad as he can make them.

His strength is an insult to the crowd. It exposes their smallness, their ridiculousness. Their disdain swells into anger. They press closer. Their projectiles become more vicious. Discarded cobblestones. Broken blocks of brick.

Every so often, one lands with a dull thump of flesh, a quiet crack of bone. The merman begins to sway with the force of the blows. His feet falter.

One of the men – a shopkeeper, Mrs Matthews thinks – pushes his way to the front of the mob. There is something unwieldy in his right hand. A rock, heavy and jagged. His muscles flex as he palms it lazily, tests its weight.

She is too far away to do anything but scream as he lifts it, swinging it with full force at the merman's head.

But Mr Matthews is closer than her. If only barely.

So it is Mr Matthews who has time to rush over, to stand in front of the merman and shelter him with an outstretched arm. It is Mr Matthews who is standing in the merman's place when the rock falls.

Mrs Matthews can only watch as it catches her husband's head, striking him at full force.

His body looks softer than it ought to, she thinks; there is something a little obscene about the plushness of the wound, the way his skull gives way like a pillow, the sumptuous velvet-red of the blood. His mouth hangs slack, and one of his pupils is blown, gaping.

Then he falls. He lands as a small, crumpled pile just beside the car.

The shopkeeper drops the rock almost instantly. It lands on the gravel, slick with blood. He falters, his hands frozen awkwardly at his sides. His eyes are very wide; he does not even seem to be breathing.

Then he bolts. Even at war, she has never seen anybody run so fast.

She would like to call him a coward, but when she opens her mouth, the word is lost to her.

Instead, she just walks towards the place where the merman is already cradling her husband's bleeding head, looking, despite everything, exactly like a scared little boy.

Mr Matthews is already unconscious when she reaches them. He is not breathing. The nurse in her knows what all of this means, even as the wife in her refuses the thought.

The car park has emptied almost entirely. It's funny how a tragedy will do that.

Only one man lingers now, a few metres behind them. He keeps shuffling backwards and forwards, as though he can't decide whether he wants to help or not, or, more charitably, as if he can't figure out whether he *can* help or not.

It's odd, but the doctor seems almost *embarrassed.*

After a while – a long emptiness punctuated by their quiet sobs and frantic, shallow breaths – he speaks up.

'We—' The pair of them turn to look, and his courage almost fails him. He tries again. 'We should call an ambulance,' he says. 'They can help us move – they can help. They'll know what to do.'

Nobody springs to action. They both just stare at him. So he steps forward, reaching out a hand as if to move Mr Matthews.

The merman's reaction is ferocious and instant. In less than a second, his hand is on top of the doctor's, holding it off with a death grip, teeth bared and snarling. For the first time, he is behaving exactly like the creature the villagers all imagine him to be.

Mrs Matthews looks at him, puzzled, her brow knitted. He doesn't snarl at her, of course, but he does shake his head softly, moving her hand gently to the side.

He stands and scoops Mr Matthews into his arms, cradling him. The old man looks suddenly like a tiny, sleeping child.

The merman sets off, out of the car park. His pace is fast – faster than usual – but still steady enough that Mrs Matthews can stay close behind him.

As they walk, she sees the gaping sores on his back, the here-and-there places where blood is still trickling down and carving strange patterns into his skin. The fresh bruises on his shoulders, his neck, around his eye sockets.

She's reminded of how very pale he looked in the crypt; all at once, she notices his bare feet on the road, how the extra weight is pressing them down and blanching them at the joints.

He's making it look easy, his strength rendering Mr Matthews insubstantial, hollow-boned. But he isn't really, of course, and the merman is injured. The pain, Mrs Matthews reasons, must be extraordinary.

Yet the merman is marching ever onwards, down the cliff road towards the sea, as if his very life depends on it. Gone is his wandering gaze, eyes roaming to study every element of this strange new world. Now, he is single-minded to an almost frightening degree. Mrs Matthews thinks that the ocean itself could not stop him.

She is proven right, because, when they reach the water's edge, the merman carries right on as if he hasn't seen it, the rocking waves hardly slowing his pace as he marches her husband's body into the surf. She hesitates for only half a second – if that – before she wades in after them.

The water slows her down, and so the merman is ahead of her when he stops. She can only see his back, an immense scarred wall, impervious to the tide and the swell of the waves. Then he stoops over, his spine curling, his figure hunched. His shoulders spasm up and down, just slightly, as though he's shivering.

It is only when she is able to wade alongside him that she realises what's really happening.

The merman is crying.

Great, heavy tears like molten silver, pouring from his eyes and onto Mr Matthews's body. They had both thought that the merman couldn't cry, not liquid tears like this; in all the time they have known him, all the sickness and all the pain, he has never shed a single tear.

Now he sobs as though his very soul will break, and the tears are staining great trails down his cheeks, and she can hear each one of them land, forceful, on Mr Matthews's skin.

She is so struck by the sight that it takes her a long while to realise what his tears are doing – that is, that they're *doing something* to her husband.

Each time a tear hits him, it's burrowing into his skin, like molten embers vanishing into snow, carving its silvery trail *into* his body somehow.

In these wounds, starting to grow and bud, are tiny pearlescent structures: glimmering barnacles and limpets, a baby starfish, alive and twitching.

Where the merman holds Mr Matthews's body in the water, floating it, the sea seethes and foams around them as if to answer his agitation. It's painful to look at, because each wave that strikes the old man animates him, swelling his limbs here and there, lending a living sheen to his skin. The way he rises and falls, it could almost seem as though he were breathing.

A tremendous swell comes then, a wave which engulfs them all in white foam, lifts and threatens to tumble them. For a moment, her husband's body bobs away, out of the merman's grip, and she cries out, certain that he is gone, that she will never see him again.

But then his head pops up beside her. He gasps. Breathless, laughing. Very much alive.

The merman turns to her next. His extraordinary eyes are still heavy and sodden with tears, peering out at her from that wild, bearded face. He raises his vast, tear-kissed hands to her neck and rests them there, heavy and warm and getting warmer by the second, until she feels a fierce burning, until she is sure she will be singed.

She feels the change the moment it happens: the gills swelling under her skin like glands in a flu, growing solid and hot and then erupting in a spectacular tearing aside of skin. She can feel the lenses of her eyes stiffening, can feel the moment that the cold wind and flecks of the sea stop stinging them, when they are hard and lodged in their sockets. She feels the saltwater racing in her blood, seeping cold around her bones. Can feel herself swell and loosen with it.

Soon, she is something else entirely.

Before she goes, she turns once more to the shore. The doctor is there, watching, one hand lifted to his brow to guard against the sun.

He is so very small from here. Shrinking by the second as they drift further away.

Mrs Matthews looks up to the cliffs. If she searches carefully, she can see her kitchen window glimmering where it catches the midday light. She says a silent good-bye to it all – to the house, the village, the only world that they have known.

Then she takes her husband's hand, and they follow their merman to the place where all strange, outcast things must be carried in the end. To the sea.

Acknowledgements

These acknowledgements took me a long time to write. The people who have supported me on this journey are so numerous, and so extraordinary, that once I started writing about them, I found I couldn't stop. I could write another whole book about the people who helped me create this one.

A huge thank you to my agent, David Godwin, for his unfailing generosity and dedication. I will be forever grateful to him for showing such confidence in me as a young, new writer, and for leading me into the literary world. *Monstrum* would not exist without his encouragement and care. Thanks also to the whole DGA team: Rachel Taylor, Heather Godwin, Sebastian Godwin, Philippa Sitters and Aparna Kumar.

Thank you to my editor, Juliet Mabey, who so instinctively 'got' my stories from the very beginning, and who has been the most insightful and supportive collaborator an author could wish for. She has been such a warm and thoughtful presence throughout every part of this process – I never imagined I could enjoy receiving feedback so much!

Oneworld has been the best home imaginable for my debut book. Thank you to everyone else on the team who has worked so hard to bring *Monstrum* to life: my fantastic copyeditor, Helen Szirtes, Polly Hatfield in Editorial, Hayley Warnham and Ben Summers in Design, Paul Nash and Laura Mcfarlane in Production, Mark Rusher, Lucy Cooper and Mary Hawkins in Marketing, Kate Appleton and Matilda Warner in Publicity, Julian Ball and Francesca Dawes in Sales and Anne Bihan in Rights.

Thank you to the BBC Young Writers' Award for starting me off on my journey, and particularly to Claire Shanahan and Di Speirs for their continued support.

Thank you to all those authors who have been kind enough to offer me words of encouragement and advice over the years: Jenn Ashworth, Ali Smith, Ingrid Persaud, Katherine Rundell, Malorie Blackman, Will Hill, Raymond Antrobus and Liz Kessler.

Thank you to Newnham College, Cambridge, where these stories were born. Thank you in particular to Dr Bonnie Lander Johnson for introducing me to my first changeling.

Thank you to Rebecca Cox, who is simply wonderful, and without whom this book could not exist.

Thank you to my friends. To Ella Muir, who possesses a near encyclopaedic knowledge of fashion history, folk songs and selkies – and somehow manages, amidst all this, to be one of the most outstandingly kind and humble people I have ever had the pleasure of knowing. Watching her apply her costume design talents to 'The Selkie' has been a particular honour. To Katia Allen, who is somehow still the human embodiment of a warm hug even now that we are living miles apart, and whose unexpectedly wicked sense of humour has been a constant source of joy throughout this whole process. To Clara Foster, for all the 2 a.m. chats, the immensely forceful cheerleading, the motivational speeches and endless advice – an incredible champion and an even more incredible friend.

A very, very big thank you to all of those friends who have encouraged me, supported my work, made me laugh or scooped me up in the difficult times – Han Doherty, Sidsel Størmer, Riona Millar, Bethan Holloway-Strong, Reyah Martin, Francesca Holt, Molly Bear and Hannah Levene, to name but a few. You are all remarkable.

So many of the stories in *Monstrum* are a love letter to extraordinary families. I could not have written them if I myself did not come from the most remarkable and loving family imaginable.

An immense thank you to all the extended family and family friends who have been so enthusiastic and supportive of me and my work – it means more than I can say.

Thank you to Nanny, who has looked after me always,

in every possible way, and Grandad, who has fuelled my imagination with midnight mermaid-seeking expeditions and tales of bloodthirsty pirates.

Thank you to Nana, a brilliantly effusive supporter, whose delightfully enthusiastic reactions to good news I always look forward to, and Grandad Jason, whose superhuman warmth and kindness have been a constant source of support throughout my life.

Thank you to my brother-in-law James, one of the loveliest people I have ever met, who I am giddy to be able to call part of our family. Thank you to my gorgeous nephew Archer, who is joy personified, and whose arrival was the best moment of my life so far.

Thank you to my beautiful big sister, Milly, the best protector, ally and partner-in-crime a little sister could wish for. Milly is the strongest person I know, kind and fierce and funny, and I will never be able to express just how much I love and look up to her.

Thank you to my lovely dad, who has carried me throughout my life, figuratively and, very often, literally – over beaches, rivers, fields and, on several memorable occasions, up mountains – who has ensured, at every turn, that my experience would be an extraordinary one. He has loved me so much, with such incredible warmth and determination, and I couldn't love him more.

Thank you to my mum, who is magic – a healer, storyteller and mind-reader – who knows me far better than I know myself, and who has never faltered in her belief that difference should be embraced and celebrated. My mum is the most profoundly kind person I have ever met, wise, warm, witty and strong – put simply, the most extraordinary mother imaginable. I love her 'more than the sun loves its shine'.

You are all exactly the family I would have chosen for myself. None of this would be possible without you.

© Jojo Barlow

Lottie Mills was born in Hampshire and grew up in West Sussex, Hertfordshire, and Essex. She studied English at Newnham College, Cambridge, and contributed to *Varsity* and *The Mays* during her time there. In 2020, she won the BBC Young Writers' Award for her short story 'The Changeling', having been previously shortlisted in 2018. Her work has been broadcast on BBC Radio 1 and BBC Radio 4, and she has appeared on programmes including *Look East*, *Life Hacks* and *Woman's Hour* to discuss her writing. *Monstrum* is her debut book.